MISTLETOE MISCHIEF

A LOST AND FOUND SERIES NOVELLA- ROGER

J.M. MADDEN

MISTLETOE MISCHIEF

BY

J.M. Madden

COPYRIGHT

A NOTE FROM THE AUTHOR~

When I put Duncan's book out, the manuscript had been cleaned a good bit, but there had been some character threads cut that I just couldn't bear to get rid of. Roger was one of those. He started as a scene, but I realized he needed to be much more. He was such a good hearted guy, he needed his own love story, not just a mention.
Gabe was the same way. And I wanted to continue on with Zeke and his family as well.
I hope you enjoy these glimpses into their lives!

If you'd like to connect with me on social media and keep updated on my releases, try these links:
Newsletter
Website
Facebook
Twitter

And of course you can always email me at
authorjmmadden@gmail.com

To my dedicated readers. I love and appreciate every single one of you! And I love the enthusiasm you have for these men. You keep them as real to me in my mind as my own kids.
To my gorgeous husband. I'll do another twenty with you babe!
Mayas, Karen and Sandie, you guys humble me with your patience, time and honest opinion. Thank you for being such great cheerleaders!
Dahlia Rose, thank you for the insult you gave me permission to use! I love it!!!
Meg, fabulous job! Seriously!
And to all military— current, past and future— be safe and thank you for everything that you do!

ROGER

CHAPTER ONE

ROGER LOOKED AROUND at the crazy ass lights strung throughout the room at the Frog Dog bar, but they didn't shine nearly as bright as the woman beside him.

As far as he was concerned, Cassandra Jones was the epitome of every black man's dream. Lush, unblemished, golden caramel skin glowed in the soft light of the bar, but her eyes sparkled like diamonds. They were unique, toffee gold shot with shards of antique jade, and deeper than they seemed. He'd never seen anything like them. Her gaze followed his every movement as if she couldn't look away.

Roger was used to being looked at. Between the pros-thetic myoelectric right arm and the heavy scars on his neck, there was a lot to look at. Used to be women would scope him out because he was damn hot, but he didn't believe that was the case anymore. As realistic as the arm prosthetic was, it still stood out like a sore thumb, no pun and no lie.

But... Cassandra didn't seem to mind the prosthetic. She'd explored every inch of it she could see, asking him questions about the realistic looking thermoplastic skin of his hand and the way the elbow joint moved, how strong the grip was. The arm itself was cutting edge technology and the updated electrodes made the movements more natural. He was very thankful that he'd been in the beta program to test it out through the local VA hospital.

Roger answered everything as naturally as he could, though he watched for anything negative in her intelligent eyes. It wasn't everyday you met a man that had had his arm blown off by an IED. But so far he'd only seen honest curiosity in her expression.

He'd gotten very used to seeing the negative. Any time he was out on the street, some idiot had to make a big deal about his arm. The really special, super sensitive snowflakes just *had* to turn his disability into a political issue and that really pissed him off. He'd gotten very good at raising the middle finger on his prosthetic hand.

Cassandra leaned into his line of sight. "Where did you go?"

"Sorry, baby. You're taking all of this," he lifted his arm slightly, "very well. Why is that?"

She shrugged and glanced down the bar. Chad had just come out in that damn Santa suit and was playing up to the little ones. Cassandra smiled as she watched them, her eyes sad.

"My little brother Andre was killed in Afghanistan three years ago. Friendly fire accident. He'd only been in the Army a couple of years."

Roger winced. "Oh, damn. I'm sorry."

She shrugged again. "He knew it was dangerous when he went in, but he still did it. He wanted to get out of our old neighborhood, so he did. And besides," she continued, taking a swallow of beer, "I get looks all the time for my size. I don't throw stones. Everybody has something they're insecure about."

Roger frowned, mystified. "What about your size? I think you're fucking beautiful."

She snorted, looking at him out of the corners of her eyes. "Yeah, whatever."

Daring to reach out, knowing he was probably overstepping his first-date bounds, he took her chin into his left hand and looked her in the eye. "I think you're beautiful," he told her firmly.

There was a flicker of something in her gaze, like the night had just taken on a different kind of connotation. Had she expected him to just blow her off? Had men actually treated her like that before?

Such somber thoughts for a first date.

"So how did you get my name?" he asked finally.

After a long, pregnant moment, she grinned fully for the first time since she'd sat down and Roger had to catch his breath. It had been a long time since he'd basked in that kind of sunshine. "A friend of mine talked to you at work and thought we would be a good pair. I work at the advertising company next door to Baker and Company."

"Ah, okay," Roger nodded. "Yeah, we worked a case there not too long ago. Somebody was helping themselves to the electronics the company was developing."

Cassandra hummed in agreement, tucking her curly black hair behind her ear. It just brushed her shoulders. Roger noticed that she had two ear piercings down low, and one up higher in the shell of her ear. A diamond winked in the light. It was in a place that he wanted to tease.

"Yes, and being a start-up," she told him, "they didn't have the money to lose if that prototype had been complete. You guys did a good job catching him."

Roger could tell her he had been the one who had put the details together, but he didn't want to sound boastful. "Did you know the guy that was arrested?"

3

She shook her head. "Nah. We'd done advertising for the company, but we'd worked with other people."

"Who was your friend? The set-up guru."

"Brenda Logan. She works in the front office and we like to go to lunch together. She knew I hadn't been out with anyone in a while and she was just busting at the seams to tell me about you."

Roger laughed, remembering the older woman. "The cat lady."

Cassandra laughed and nodded. "Oh, yes, the cat lady. I think she's slimmed down her herd but she still has way too many."

"She seemed to have a good heart though."

Her smile softened. "Yes, she does. A tremendous heart. And though her personal life is not as full as it should be, she's a fabulous judge of character. She told me you had the heart of a tiger and would catch the person responsible."

Roger laughed at the comparison. "I don't know about a tiger."

"Well," Cassandra cautioned, "just remember this is the cat lady. Everything revolves around cats one way or another."

Roger couldn't remember enjoying a conversation more, even though it was pretty mundane. "I'm glad you called me. This has been totally enjoyable."

She blinked at him and frowned. "You know, you're absolutely right. You don't have fifty-eight relatives living in your two-bedroom apartment, do you? Or ten pit bulls in your back yard?"

Roger shook his head. "Nope, sorry."

"Criminal record?"

He shook his head again. "Squeaky clean."

"Paying child support to six kids by seven different mothers?"

Laughing, he shrugged lightly. "I would love to be a father someday, but no. What can I say? I'm a good guy."

She scowled theatrically, eyeing him up and down. "You sound too good to be true. I better snatch you up. Wanna get married?"

Laughing out loud, skin tingling from her perusal, he smacked the bar with his good hand. "Hot damn, woman. You're some kind of wonderful. Yes, I'll marry you."

A considering, thoughtful light entered her eyes and she tipped her chin up. "I don't know about marriage, yet, but you definitely earned a second date."

Roger shuddered dramatically to make her laugh, but inside he was enormously thrilled with the progress of the night. Maybe he wasn't a total lost cause after all.

∽

CASSANDRA STARED AT THE DELICIOUS, model perfect man sitting beside her on the barstool. She couldn't help herself. Roger Stottsberry was a real, honest to goodness *gentleman*. A damned handsome gentleman, no less. Kind of took a girl off guard to be treated so nicely, especially when she wasn't used to it.

Cass forced her gaze to look away. She didn't know any of these people circling the room, but they had welcomed her with open arms, some of them literally. Roger was obviously well-liked in this group and they seemed surprised and genuinely happy when she'd shown up to be his date for the Christmas Eve party.

It made her wonder *why* they'd been so surprised.

"Are you gay?"

Roger choked on the swallow of beer he'd just taken. "What?"

Cass clamped her mouth shut as he swiveled toward her.

Thick, muscular thighs were braced on the supports of the stool and his dark jeans were tight across his hips, leaving her in no doubt of what he carried in there. The man wore a nice T-shirt under a button down red and blue checked flannel shirt, tucked into his waistband. She wanted to make a joke about moobs and cleavage, but she worried that he would realize how fascinated she was with the center line between his heavy pectoral muscles. Not a lot of hair, which was fine with her. Damn she wanted to explore, though. A curl of arousal lit low in her tummy and she really, *really* hoped he wasn't gay.

Roger glared at her incredulously, as if he couldn't believe what she'd asked.

Cass shrugged. "Do you blame me for thinking it? You're too pretty not to be."

Roger tipped back his head and laughed deeply, his whole chest moving with the emotion. Several people looked their way, smiling, and she felt a little embarrassed at drawing attention.

Then, his laughter slowly faded. He turned back to face forward, bracing his elbows on the bar as he held the beer bottle between his hands. He seemed to be looking at the prosthetic.

She didn't like feeling like she'd done something to hurt him. Leaning over, she bumped his shoulder. "Are you okay?"

With a single tip of the head, he saluted her with the beer bottle as he took a sip.

"I'm fine. Thank you for the ego stroking. It's been a while."

"I meant every word."

There was a shuffle at the bar as the big guy with the terribly scarred face grabbed a fresh beer from the cooler beneath the bar.

Roger seemed happy for the interruption.

"How's he doing, Zeke?" Roger asked, voice hushed.

The big guy paused for a moment, bright blue eyes shining. "Not too b-b-b-bad. You can tell he's a little rusty."

Cass thought she heard Roger mutter 'aren't we all' under his breath and almost laughed.

With a broad smile, Zeke hustled over to the booth on the far side of the room. A man and a woman sat there, pretty much just staring at each other. The older guy finished off his beer and Zeke dropped the new one in front of him almost seamlessly.

Cass chuckled a little. It was obvious the two in the booth had been set up as well, and you could almost *see* the attraction between them. "There's a lot of tension in here tonight, and not just because of the holiday."

Roger glanced at her out of the corner of his eye. "You have no idea."

Reaching out, she ran a fingernail down over the bulge of deltoid muscle in his right shoulder. She stopped at the edge of the prosthetic, then circled around part way. She didn't understand why she had to touch him. It was very unlike her. But something about the night or the setting made her feel a little … reckless.

Roger gave her that look again, his dark eyes hooded and wary.

Cass drew her finger back, thinking she'd dared enough, and picked up her drink. Her heart raced, giving lie to her calm movements. She hoped Roger couldn't tell how excited she was.

As she'd gotten ready for this party, she'd changed her clothes literally *ten times*, all in the hope of finding something, *anything*, that would make her look skinnier. Somewhat disappointingly, it didn't happen. So, she went with a cable knit black sweater, a slinky red camisole visible in the deep V neckline of the sweater. Fancy blue jeans with a little bling on the ass pockets finished off the combo. Comfortable to wear and warm enough when she needed to go out. Okay, and the cut of the sweater made her boobs look good, too, but it didn't matter. It wasn't like anything would come of this date anyway.

She remembered seeing Roger a couple weeks ago, going into the business next door to hers, so tall and strong. He'd been dressed casually in low-slung jeans and a button down shirt. In her heart, she knew he wouldn't be into her. As beautiful as he was, he would take one look at her and relegate her to the 'friends' category. Or if he did actually want to fuck her, he'd wait until they were in the parking lot, away from his own friends, before he let her know. One of her exes had flat out told her she had the kind of shape he liked to fuck, but he'd never stay with her.

Because it just wouldn't be good to be seen with a girl as big as she was.

Now that she was here and actually talking with Roger, she started to think that she'd been wrong assuming he'd be like other men she'd known. Things weren't going the way she'd expected at all, so she could only guess.

There was a burst of chatter from the front of the restaurant and she realized people were looking out the windows. The snow had begun to fall harder outside. The group seemed to be moving to wrap things up.

"I don't want to leave yet," she murmured.

Roger gave her a look, and she could tell he was once again trying to size her up.

"What?" she asked defensively. "I like your people. And I like you. It's been a long time since I've been out and haven't had to threaten to call the cops on my date."

Roger's eyebrows shot up on his forehead and she nodded. "Yep. Last two, anyway. Furry faced, web-footed, octopus mother effers."

He chuckled at her look, or her words, she couldn't tell. She only cared that she'd made him laugh.

Cass stared at his eyes, trying to see the bad. All men had something bad about them. Some men were all bad, others had just a little bit, but they all hid it well. She just couldn't tell with Roger. He *seemed* like a gentleman. But she'd thought that before.

None of the other men she'd been with had been in the Marines though. Maybe the military had had a redeeming affect on him. It definitely had for her brother.

In the deepest, most protected corner of her heart she hoped he was as real as he seemed.

Roger had turned to look out the windows of the bar. "Did you drive here?" he asked, turning back to her.

Nodding, she looked out the windows again, praying that the damn snow would stop. She'd seen the weather forecast, though, and it hadn't sounded good. She didn't want this evening to end. "Yes," she sighed. "I drove."

Not like she'd *not* have a car out here, living on her own. Damn she was feeling defensive right now. Was that because he had her emotions so off kilter?

Around them, the group had begun to pack up, the wrapping paper trash picked up and food being wrapped up for safe transport home. There were several people in a huddle over by Roger's good looking boss. The woman with the striking auburn hair spoke a few words, then seemed surprised the direction the conversation went but she eventually nodded.

"I hate to rush you off," Roger said finally, "but I think the weather has taken a turn for the worse."

Dammit.

"Yes, looks like it," she agreed.

She looked at him again, resigned. Tonight had been an aberration for her, on many different levels. It had been a whimsical, intriguing interlude in her not-so-easy life. "I enjoyed being here tonight, Roger."

He smiled a little playfully. "I did too, Miss Cassandra."

Cass waited a moment, hoping he would ask her out, or over for coffee or something, but he didn't. Instead he slid off the stool and reached for the weather gear on the stool beside him. Cass stepped off as well and looped her scarf around her neck, trying not to show her disappointment. When she reached for her coat, he already stood behind her, holding it out. With a little thrill, she reached her arms into the coat and turned to face him, her heart hammering with anticipation. He stood a few inches over six feet, the perfect kissing height.

They were inches apart and for a brief moment he looked like he wanted to lower his head and kiss her, then he blinked, clamped his square jaw and pulled away.

"I'll walk you out."

Cass gritted her teeth. She'd seen that flash of interest in his eyes a couple of times tonight. What the hell did she need to do to get him to commit to something, even something as simple as a kiss?

Then it hit her. Maybe he *wouldn't* kiss her. Maybe she'd misread everything and this was a goodbye walk.

They each had their insecurities, that much was obvious.

Cass said her goodbyes to the nice women she'd met and walked out of the restaurant, Roger on her heels. She could feel his gaze on her and as she stepped off the curb to the parking lot, he was there to offer her his elbow.

He'd given her his real arm. She tightened her hand on his elbow and thought about leaning her head on his shoulder as they walked into the snow, but she didn't let herself do that. This was going to be the big brush-off scene, she'd played it out before.

She pointed out her car and they moved toward it. At one

point she slipped a little, but he tightened his arm and braced to hold her.

"You okay, baby?"

Her heart clenching from the words more than the threat of a painful fall, Cass wanted to turn to him and wrap her arms around him. He had done absolutely everything right. He'd been more solicitous of her than any other man ever had. There was an aching sadness to him that she wanted to make better. Even as he smiled at her through the falling flakes, he seemed... overwhelmed by life. Sad. As if what he wanted was too far out of his reach.

Was she actually seeing that or was she seeing what she *wanted* to see?

This was so frustrating. Maybe she just needed to lay it out there.

"Roger, I want to see you again."

Cass didn't even realize she'd spoken until his eyes widened. Then, with a sad smile, he shook his head. "I'll follow you home to make sure you get there okay, but that's all, Cassandra. That's all I can give you tonight."

Reaching up, she ran her fingers down his cheek, then down the scarred side of his neck, feeling the texture of the old hurt. He didn't move, but she could feel him withdraw emotionally. Then he stepped back from her and she let her fingers fall to her side.

She'd known this man exactly one evening, just a few hours. She'd never behaved this way with another man in her life, but she feared that if she let him go tonight she wouldn't see him again.

Everything she had in her life now was because she'd dared to reach for it. So, following her instincts, she cupped Roger's neck in her hand and drew him down toward her. Their lips met with the slightest brush, then another. Cass inhaled against his mouth, angled her head then sealed her lips against his.

Now, if he'd truly been against the kiss, he would have drawn away, but he didn't. For a timeless moment, she feared that she would be the only one involved, because he didn't move for such a terribly long time. It was probably only a couple of seconds but it felt like so much more. Then, suddenly, he cupped her face in his hands.

Cass had kissed many frogs in her life, but every single asshole with hurtful hands and nauseating breath and bring-you-down-drama went out of her mind just then. Roger made her heart race. Tingles shot down her body and she dared to reach for his shoulders to hold on. She didn't want to leave his delicious mouth.

But he jerked away. Not just away from her mouth but completely away from her body.

Cass blinked her eyes open in shock, wondering what she'd done wrong.

"Are you okay?" she asked, voice breathless.

He blinked at her, his expressive eyes hidden by the shadows cast by the parking lot security light. "Yes, I'm fine," he told her voice gruff. "You should get home, though. It's getting late."

Frowning, she tried to read his face but he seemed to be deliberately averting it from her. She turned away with a huff, tears filling her eyes. But she would not let them fall. "Sorry I wasted your time tonight, Roger."

Without another word she slipped into her Hyundai and pulled the seatbelt across her lap. The car started, after a slight hesitation. Making sure he'd moved away, she backed out of the parking space and left the restaurant parking lot.

CHAPTER TWO

ROGER'S HEART was thudding in his chest, and it wasn't something he was comfortable with or had ever expected. Cassandra Jones had just rocked his world with a simple kiss.

For the life of him though, he couldn't tell if she was did it because she wanted to or because she felt sorry for him. He felt like they'd clicked in the bar, but it had been so long since he'd had any real interaction with women.

Almost all of his buddies around him had found that significant other. Was he *hoping* there was more to this attraction?

The first woman he'd been with after he'd gotten home from surgical rehab had felt sorry for him. At the time he'd been so hard up for sex and confirmation that he could still perform like a man, he hadn't cared. He'd left his shirt on and pounded her into orgasm after orgasm in the dark of the room. Later, thinking back on his actions, he decided he'd been motivated to prove to her how much of a man he was, even with only one arm. He'd seen the shiver go through her body, though, when he'd touched her with his prosthetic. And it hadn't been a good shiver.

That had been several years ago, and he'd vowed not to be with another woman until he felt like she was the right one. The one woman who'd see *him*, Roger, not just the remains of his injuries.

With a sinking heart, he felt like the right one just drove out of the parking lot and he had let her go.

Tonight, Cassandra had shined a light into his barren heart. She'd teased him and enticed him into conversation, a little flirting even, and seemed to be a good-hearted soul. Her angel's wings might be a little tattered, but she was stronger for it, and continued to move forward in life. He admired that. He admired *her*. He didn't want this interaction with the rusty side of his social skills to make her stumble on the path to reaching her goals.

With a wince, he headed to his Jeep. Kicking it into four-wheel drive he followed the path she'd left in the snow. It wasn't long until he caught up with her. She was driving very carefully along the streets, leaving herself plenty of braking room, but she was still skidding a little. The car would jerk occasionally on ice, then level out. In all honesty, though, she was driving like she actually had a brain in her head compared to the rest of the idiots out here. The snow hadn't been coming down long, but there were already vehicles in ditches.

When she pulled up in front of a cookie cutter apartment block, he parked right behind her. Then he hesitated, gripping the steering wheel in indecision, he didn't know what he was going to say, but she needed some kind of explanation for his strange behavior.

Unfortunately, when he climbed out of his Jeep she stood right there waiting for him. "Why the hell are you following me home? Do you think this is the first time I've ever driven in snow? I can guarantee you it's not, I've lived in Denver my whole life."

"I know you can," he growled. "That's not why I followed you. I needed to apologize."

That set her back on her heels. "Oh," she said quietly, crossing her arms. Her puffy blue coat seemed to make that a little hard to do, but she managed. Her breath huffed out in clouds in the cold air. In the scant light from the parking lot, her eyes seemed red-rimmed and guarded. Cassandra had one of the strongest personalities he'd ever encountered. The thought that he'd upset her didn't sit well with him. She deserved better.

The snow continued to fall, landing in her curly hair. Roger wanted to reach out and tug at those curls, but in this mood she'd probably slap his hand away.

"I'm sorry I didn't respond to you the way I should have," he told her after a few seconds.

She shrugged, burrowing her chin into the collar of the winter coat. "No skin off my nose."

He sighed. "Are you always this defensive? Why won't you let me talk?"

Her mouth snapped shut and she cocked her head at him, as if waiting.

"It's been a very long time since I've been on any kind of date," he told her finally. "Like, years. Years. I guarantee you that I used to be a very different man. You took me by surprise tonight."

She seemed shocked at the admission. And even though the sentences were disjointed she seemed to understand what he was telling her.

"I'm sorry I rushed you then," she said softly.

Roger looked out at the night, and the brightly twinkling Christmas lights around them. They were all alone on the street and the sounds of passing traffic were muffled. Snow covered the streets and houses and cars. Roger suddenly had a childhood memory of waking up and finding out that school had been cancelled. Time was passing, and he'd not realized how fast until tonight.

"I'm kind of glad you rushed me, actually," he told her. "I think I needed it."

He turned back to her and dared to take a step closer. "Did you kiss me because you felt sorry for me?"

Her face clouded with anger and impatience. "What?"

He held up his hand. "Never mind. Your response tells me what I wanted to know. I just don't want to be some man you think needs to be pitied and coddled."

Cassandra took a deep breath and glanced down at her feet. When she finally looked back up at him, there were tears glittering in her eyes, but her expression told him that she didn't want pity either. "You know, we're both defensive and cautious. For a minute I dared to hope that you were the nice, normal kind of guy I've always been looking for. I grew up on the streets, literally, I mean. Everything I have, I've worked my ass off for. But I got myself away from everything bad. Or at least, I've tried my damnedest to. Seems like the bad finds me, whether I want it to or not. You're the first guy that doesn't feel bad to me."

Roger gave her a crooked smile, in spite of the wild emotions roiling up in his heart. "I'm a man, Cassandra. I'm liable to mess up here and there, but you never have to worry about your safety with me. I was raised better than that. My parents made sure to teach me to be a man that respects women, and I can tell you that I respect *everything* about you so far."

Her throat tightened with emotion and her eyes teared up, but she didn't let them fall. Roger reached out and brushed his thumbs down her cheeks. "I want another chance to kiss you, Cassandra. Can I do that?"

After a long, drawn out moment, she nodded, and he didn't give her a chance to change her mind. Leaning down, his heart racing, he fit his lips to hers. He tasted the tears she finally let fall, and it made him sad, even as he thrilled to her touch. If he had it in his power, he wanted to make the sadness weighing both of them down go away.

Cassandra leaned into him and reached up to cup his face. And when he drew back enough to look at her, she smiled at him, her unique eyes now clear and determined. "I don't know if it's because of the Christmas spirit or what, but I want you to come home with me. Even if we just sit on the couch and talk, I don't care. I just don't want to break this spell yet."

Roger felt the same way. "I couldn't have said it better myself."

He locked his vehicle and waited as she retrieved her purse and phone from her own car. Then, hand in hand, they walked along the snow-covered pavement to the entrance to her building. They climbed the steps to the second floor, and he held her purse as she unlocked the door to her apartment.

Roger couldn't get enough of touching her. He helped her remove her coat and hung it on the wall next to the door, then slowly drew the scarf from around her neck. There was a satisfied smile on her face that he loved, and he wanted it to stay there all night just so that he could look at it. The tears were gone and he wanted them to stay gone.

"Can I get you something to drink?" she asked him eventually, when the silence stretched out. "I'm a little chilled and in the mood for hot chocolate."

Roger grinned. "I haven't had hot chocolate for years. That sounds perfect for tonight."

Cassandra turned to walk away, and he allowed himself to watch her go. She was not a skinny woman, not by any means, and her body made him salivate. She had a body built to satisfy a man, with substantial hips and breasts that would spill over his hands. Roger wanted to explore her and find what made her happy, what made her giggle. He especially wanted to know what would make her cry out his name in pleasure. Just the thought made his body harden. He'd been fighting it all night, but every time she'd touched him his blood had heated.

It was too soon to be this attracted to her. He shook his head and tried to regain control of himself again.

"Make yourself at home," she called to him from the kitchen.

Roger took her at her word and after kicking his boots off at the door, walked into her living room. The entire space wasn't very big, looked to only be a single bedroom. Pretty spare but the furniture was well-made and clean. There was a small, two-foot Christmas tree on a table by the window. Not very big, but it glittered with lights and tinsel.

The tree made him sad, because it didn't sound like she had any family around since her brother had died. She'd put the tree up in spite of the fact that no one would see it except her. Another important insight into her heart. She was hopeful. And she believed in Christmas spirit.

There was a wall of framed photos, dedicated to a young man, obviously her brother. Some of the pics were of earlier years, hanging out with friends, but as Roger moved across the wall the young man changed, and the focus of his life sharpened. There was a graduation picture in maroon cap and gown where he stood proudly holding up his diploma, Cass stood beside him beaming. Roger thought she looked just as proud as the young man.

There was another picture of him standing beside a sporty red car, keys in hand, pride shining in his young face. Then there were pictures of basic training. Looked like he had been sent to Ft. Leonard Wood in Missouri. And it looked like Andre had fit in well, from the story he read the pictures on the wall.

When young men left an urban environment, it was a real shock to the system to be thrust into the dirt and sweat and pain of basic training. Roger was glad that Andre had apparently done well.

At the end of the cluster of pictures were two that made his stomach clench in recognition of shared experiences he and Andre had each had, separate places, separate times but the same even so. They were of Andre in Afghanistan. In the first he was dismantling an M4 carbine, and laughing at someone out of camera view. He'd been a good-looking young man. Basic had slimmed him down and given his strong face definition.

In the second picture it took him a minute to find Andre, because he was standing with about ten other men in complete desert gear in front of a Humvee, weapons held loosely at their sides.

Roger had a picture very similar on his own wall. When you fought overseas like that, the men you fought with became your family. You wanted to commemorate those good times, to balance out the bad.

The date at the bottom of that last picture was a little over three years ago. It must have been taken just before Andre died. What a terrible loss.

Roger circled back around the room and sank down onto the comfortable looking couch. Oh, yeah, he could totally chill here.

Cassandra made little noises as she worked, and he thought she might have been humming something. Pans clinked and water ran. Then he heard a refrigerator door open and close. He realized she was making the cocoa from scratch. Damn. Now that was dedication ... and would be delicious.

Roger sighed as the couch wrapped around him, making his eyelids heavy. The anxiety and tension from anticipating the blind date and then the actual meet up faded away. He hadn't realized how stressed he'd been.

The Christmas tree glittered, the only source of light in the room other than the glow from the kitchen.

He shut his eyes, just for a moment.

～

CASS PEEKED into the living room to ask him if he wanted some Bailey's Irish Cream in his mug, but she caught herself. Roger had tipped his head against the back of the couch and appeared to be asleep.

"Roger," she whispered.

He didn't move.

She tried again, a little louder. "Roger?"

Nothing.

Damn! He'd fallen asleep on her couch? She'd only been in the kitchen a few minutes.

Grinning, she returned to the kitchen to shut off the stove. He wouldn't be drinking any cocoa in the near future.

She was a little torn now though. Should she wake him up just kinda accidentally? Or should she just let him sleep?

Hmm. Maybe she'd just let him sleep. She moved to the kitchen window and looked out. Yeah, at the rate the snow was falling he probably should just hang out for a while. Both of their vehicles were covered now. He wouldn't be going anywhere safely in the near future. A little thrill went through her at the thought of having him in her apartment longer.

Tiptoeing into the living room, she snagged her favorite fluffy blanket from the recliner. Being extra gentle, she draped it over his slumbering form.

Mmm, mmm, such a good-looking man. Tall and lean, his build strong and solid, he dressed like a man should. Cass knew it was creepy, but she just stood there, staring down at him for a few minutes. Then he snuffled in his sleep. She thought he would wake for a moment, but he turned his head and burrowed into the cushion of the couch.

Grinning, she headed toward her bedroom. She would wear clothes tonight just in case the investigator decided to … investigate.

CHAPTER THREE

It was three a.m. when she got up to go pee. Then, because she couldn't help herself, she walked down the hallway to the living room.

Roger had stretched out on the couch. The blanket she'd pulled over him was hanging mostly off now, with just the corner covering his chest. The rest had puddled onto the floor. He was moving restlessly, as if he fought demons in his sleep.

Then he cried out and her heart raced with fear.

Cass clenched her hands, wondering if she should wake him up. She'd had dreams like that herself, and they were no fun. The flashbacks of men beating her, the pain. She stood there for a few moments, hoping the dream would let up, but instead it seemed to escalate. He seemed to be reliving the pain of losing his arm. He kept reaching for his right side. In the meager light she saw a tear slip from the corner of his eye to his temple, then another. God, her heart was shattering. She didn't want him to suffer with this pain.

Swallowing, she moved forward, but kept her distance. She knew enough not to touch him yet.

"Roger?"

He blinked his eyes open, but didn't seem to see anything.

"Roger!"

Roger blinked up at her in confusion. There was just enough light from the kitchen for her to make out his expression. He looked terrified.

His body jerked and he finally seemed to focus on her. "Oh, hey."

Her thudding heart began to slow with relief.

"Hey. You all right?"

His arms dropped to his lap and he looked around, obviously orienting himself. "Yes, I'm fine. Sorry, you just startled me."

He scrubbed at his eyes with his good hand. Cass moved closer to sit beside his legs on the couch. She wanted to reach out to reassure him, but didn't know if he was ready for the contact yet. "No, that was totally my bad. You were dreaming, though, and it was getting worse."

Roger looked down at the blanket, then glanced at her kind of sheepishly. "Yeah. I do that." He dropped his head back to the arm of the couch and covered his face with his prosthetic arm.

The heat of him seeped through to her hip and she shivered in the chill. "My brother used to do that," she admitted softly in the dark. "When he came home on leave, he would have terrible dreams. He would scream sometimes, too. It would wake me out of sleep. But he said there was nothing I could do for him and he never talked about it."

Roger's prosthetic hand settled on hers in her lap. "I'm sure just knowing you were there for him was a big comfort. Most men don't want to admit to that, but we get scared too. And we hope for something stronger than us to chase the nightmares away."

Cass nodded, her throat tight. "Yeah, I know how that is."

He squeezed her fingers lightly, and she noticed how much control he actually had with this arm. She ran her fingers over the cold surface. She shivered again, and he sat up behind her, urging her to her feet. "Come on, let's get you back to bed."

Cass allowed herself to be guided back down the hallway to her room. The light in her bathroom glowed softly, just bright enough that he could see to lift the blankets for her to settle in. Then he tugged them until they were smooth around her, and her feet were covered.

It was a surreal experience for Cass and her emotions were ricocheting like crazy. Adrenaline letdown. And now he was squeezing her heart. She couldn't remember any time in her life ever being tucked in like this. Other kids had gotten that buy not the Jones kids. Living on the streets, she'd been lucky if they even had a blanket. She used to sit in a ball with little Andre between her legs. She would wrap her arms and legs around him to conserve heat. Even after their mother had died and they'd been taken to an orphanage with friendly, but overworked people, she and Andre had stuck together. There'd been boys there who had known more than they should have for their age, and didn't mind sharing. Living on the streets as they had, she and Andre had seen and heard a lot of things, but these boys knew more. When one grabbed at her butt, saying something derogatory, she'd had no hesitation in bloodying his lip and kicking his ass. The streets had also taught them to protect themselves.

Cass shivered and clutched at Roger's hand as he started to turn away.

"Yeah, baby?"

"Can you just lay down with me for a while? No strings. Just… maybe we can just… well, be here for each other for a while."

After a long, timeless moment Roger circled the bed to

the other side and crawled beneath the blankets. He left his jeans on, which had to be uncomfortable, but she appreciated it. Once he was settled he lifted his good arm to her and she rolled close. She worried about letting all her weight rest on him, but he pulled her tight into the crook of his shoulder. He was so warm, and he smelled so good…

In her half-awake state, she knew this would lead to issues later, but she couldn't seem to help herself. As his warmth and protection seeped into her, some of the never-ending tension of always being on guard—and lonely —drifted away.

∾

ROGER WOKE WARM AND CONTENT, and surprisingly free of anxiety. There was a heavy weight across his chest. Blinking awake, he tilted his head to look down.

A curly mop of black hair tickled his nose, and a long, sleek arm draped across his chest.

Cassandra.

His good arm cradled her against his chest and his fingers rested against the soft skin of her neck. Oh, hell. What had they done?

As he became more aware, he realized they hadn't done anything. He still wore his jeans and shirt. Although he thought he felt a soft hand beneath the edge of the shirt.

He let his fingers play over the soft skin of her neck. They'd laid like this for a long time, he could tell. His hips were sore from not moving and his right arm was itchy from wearing the prosthetic all night.

The discomfort was minor, though, considering he'd slept for the past several hours. Once she'd pulled him into the bed with her, they'd both fallen asleep quickly.

That was very strange for him. He worked the graveyard

shift at Lost and Found, so when he did get time off, he tried to stay up through the night then sleep during the day, just like his regular schedule. Last night had been an aberration, though, for several reasons.

In his wildest imaginings, he never would have expected to fall asleep on her couch.

Then when the demons had come, she'd roused him. Her brother had dealt with similar issues, so she'd known what to do.

Taking him to bed and wrapping him in her arms had probably not been her original plan.

Cassandra shifted, her left hand gliding over the skin of his stomach. Roger tensed, wondering if there was a way to get out of the situation without embarrassing them both.

As soon as he'd realized who he cuddled in his arms, his body had gotten interested. And now, with her fingers playing against the sensitive skin of his abs, he was becoming more interested.

He shifted a tiny bit to let her know he was awake.

"Don't leave yet. I just want to lie here and enjoy this," she murmured.

"I'm fine with that. I just wanted to be sure you were awake."

"I am."

He wiggled a little, shifting positions with his hips. Not to draw attention to them, but to ease some of the tiredness.

She sighed and began to ease away, but he tightened his arm around her. "Don't move. I just had to shift my hips a bit. I don't think we've moved all night."

She eased back down against him, nodding slightly against his chest. "My body is aching too, but I hate to move. This has been so perfect. We both slept for *hours* without any dreams."

For another few minutes they just lay there, watching the

light brighten outside her apartment window. He could still see snow falling outside the gauzy curtains.

"What do you dream about, Cassandra?"

"My brother," she said immediately. "We did everything together, because our mother was usually gone. We relied on each other for everything. Even when they put us in the home after our mother died, we would sneak out of the segregated dorms to be with each other. When I turned eighteen and was graduated out of the home, it was the loneliest I've ever been in my life. I made some bad decisions and met some very bad men."

Roger didn't know if he wanted details or not. "There are a lot of them out there. I will say that. And to a young girl with no direction…"

"Yes," she sighed. "I was on a very bad path until I realized I needed to be ready for Andre when he got out of the home. I needed to be the rock for him that I hadn't had. That made me start thinking, planning. Within a couple weeks I had started a job and was looking for an apartment. About six months after that I petitioned the state to be Andre's guardian. It took months, but they approved me and when he was almost sixteen Andre came to live with me. It was one of the most joyous times I can ever remember, us being together again. We didn't have a lot of furniture or anything at first, so we would camp out on the floor."

"I'm glad you had that time with him."

She nodded against him. "Me too," she whispered.

Neither moved, as if they knew the tenuous wisps of dreams lost would fade away.

"Merry Christmas," he whispered.

Her body jerked, and she began to quiver. Roger thought he had hurt her somehow. "Baby, what's wrong?"

She eased back and turned her face up to look at him, then burrowed it into his shoulder.

Roger levered them both over until she was on her back and he on his elbow beside her. "What's wrong, Cassandra?"

Blinking, fighting tears, she seemed too overcome with emotion to utter a word. Her hands were clasped over her face, fingers rubbing at her eyes. Roger gathered her to him, pressing kisses to her hair and face. "You're breaking my heart, baby. Tell me, please."

"I just—," she gasped, then fought for control. "This is going to sound so lame, but this has been the best Christmas I've ever had."

Roger chuckled against her, relief making him a little giddy. "Damn, woman, I thought there was something seriously wrong."

She shook her head, laying back against his arm. "No. You've done everything right and I don't want this day to end. I'm afraid that when the real world intrudes it's all going to come falling down."

"Why?" he asked softly, looking into her jade-shot eyes.

Her face scrunched up a little. "Because that's the way my life seems to roll. I find something a little tiny bit good and life snatches it away from me. I'm afraid to hope for more."

Roger took her words and gave them the consideration they deserved. Then he pressed a firm kiss to her lips. "I think that, as of last night, your luck has changed."

For a moment she seemed hopeful, then her face crumpled. She started to tremble. "I don't know if I can do it."

He brushed her hair from her forehead. All of the make-up from the night before was gone, but she was still just as beautiful to him.

"What baby?"

For a long heartbeat of time, she looked him in the eye. "I don't know if I can lose you."

Roger stilled, wondering if he'd heard her correctly. The sick feeling in his stomach told him he had, and he realized the thought of leaving her absolutely gutted him as well. They'd been together an incredible ten, twelve hours, maybe not even that long, and he couldn't imagine her not being in his life. Cassandra Jones drew him like no other woman ever had. He cleared his throat, suddenly a little anxious. He knew what he wanted to say to her. It was there in his heart.

"I don't think I can lose you either," he admitted.

Her eyes widened as he leaned down to kiss her again, and he realized it was easier to show her how he felt than to articulate it into words. She opened her mouth to him as she cupped his face in her palms.

Roger could count on one hand the number of times he'd been kissed in the past few years, but he'd never in his life been kissed like this. As if the weight of dreams too long unrealized threatened to suck Cassandra under before she had a chance to transfer them to him. Roger took everything, every nibble and moan, and gave her back the same. In spite of the tears just now, he knew Cassandra was a strong woman. She'd battled her way out of poverty and heartbreak, and he wanted to be as strong as she was.

Yes, he'd been through a lot physically, but he felt like *she* was the warrior.

Roger allowed himself to feel the body beneath him. Lush and soft, Cassandra's shape was his idea of a *real* woman. Her breasts pressed against his chest, making his hands want to wander, but he didn't want to move too fast. His body was ready to go all the way, and his mind and his heart were quickly getting on board with the idea, but it was entirely up to her. He didn't want to push her into anything.

Cassandra moaned into his mouth, shuddering, and he hardened to the point of pain. Shifting his hips away from her, he tried to maintain control over his rioting body, but it was hard to do with every signal she put out telling him that she wanted him.

Then her hands clutched his ass, dragging him back over top of her. Roger gasped as she ground her pelvis up against his own.

"Oh, fuck, baby, you have to stop doing that or we'll never get out of this bed."

"And is that a bad thing? You're the first man I've wanted here in years."

He stilled and looked down at her. Those seductive eyes of hers were clear with determination and half-slitted with arousal. "Are you serious?"

She nodded, her dark hair a halo around her head. She gave him a soft, tentative smile and shrugged a little self-consciously. "Like I said, had to call cops for the last two. One wouldn't take no for an answer and tried to beat me into a yes, and the other just wanted to get close enough to steal my car. They never got anywhere near my lusciousness, though."

She grinned up at him, and that warrior spirit of hers turned self-consciousness to bravado.

Roger grinned down at her, entranced by her. "You amaze me, Cassandra Jones."

With a long, considering smile, she pushed at his chest, rolling him to his back. Then she sat up, turned to face him and whipped her sleep shirt over her head.

Roger almost choked on his tongue, not daring to believe that the beauty in front of him wanted him. He suddenly felt very insecure in his own body. Yes, he worked out and tried to eat right, but the goddess before him put all his efforts to shame, in a completely different way. She was glorious and womanly, her body rounded yet firm. She still wore a white sports bra, but it did little to hide her magnificent breasts.

In the pale light of dawn, her creamy coffee skin seemed even softer than before. Paying special attention to the feel, he ran a finger over her soft shoulder and down her arm.

He thought of the 'I'm no Angel' campaign he'd seen on TV recently. The 'plus-sized' women drew his attention more than any other advertisement he'd ever seen. Cassandra would fit into that line-up and outshine every woman there. She looked happy and healthy, not sickly like most of the super-models other men seemed to go for.

She was so beautiful to him that his throat tightened with emotion.

Then he felt a wave of self-doubt. As daring as she was pulling her shirt off like that, he didn't feel nearly as excited to whip off his own clothes. His bottom half wasn't too bad. Yeah, some scars and old burns, but his top half was a mess. And that was before you even got to the arm.

Cass took his silence as censure and began to cover herself. Roger sat up beside her, reaching out to cup her neck. "No, baby, don't you dare cover those breasts. They're superb. I was just thinking that I'm not nearly as magnificent. I look like the worn side of an old boot."

She looked down at his chest, then planted her hands on his pectorals. Her fingers began to explore, and he let her.

"I've been dreaming of exploring this chest all night," she told him softly. "You look mouth-watering. And when you wear tight T-shirts like that, you have to expect women to throw themselves at you, even with the flannel on."

He winced. "Yeah, they do, sometimes. But I shut them down because I know what I'll see in their expressions when they finally see *me*."

Cassandra frowned and looked directly into his eyes. "I know it's just words, but you can't judge me by the other women that have passed through your life. I've seen a lot of fucked up shit in my own life, but I don't think what you have under here," she plucked at the material, "will spook me nearly as bad as other things I've seen."

She pressed a soft kiss to his lips. "But I don't want to

31

guilt you into exposing yourself if you're not ready. If this relationship goes anywhere, it can't be built on sour emotions like that. You do what makes you comfortable. I want that shine back in your eyes."

She smiled at him, and he automatically smiled back, then he looked down at the expanse of cleavage in front of him and huffed out a breath. Cupping the weight of her breasts in his hands, he leaned down to press a kiss to the slope of each one. Cassandra shivered at his touch, and the banked arousal surged again. She was a delectable piece of bliss just waiting to be eaten, and he was worried about the damn scars.

Maybe he was so worried about it because he actually *could* imagine a forever with Cassandra, and he didn't want to risk the possibility of that for anything.

But then he wondered if he shouldn't go ahead and get it over with. He would rather be hurt now than weeks or months down the road when they were solidly entrenched in each other's lives.

Pulling back from her, giving her solid eye contact, he hesitated only a second, then dragged the T-shirt over his head.

Cassandra's eyes widened at his abrupt move, but she kept her gaze on his even as her smile broadened. "You make me see beauty," she told him, voice hushed. "Not of the body, but of the soul, which is much more important. I haven't had that in my life. And before you get offended at me calling you beautiful, it's just about the best compliment I can give you."

Roger blinked, then blinked again to clear the blurriness. All this damn emotion was seriously messing with his head.

Then her gaze drifted down to his shoulders. His skin prickled as she looked at the scarring. It had been several years since he'd been Medevaced out of Iraq. Most of the scars had darkened with age, but a few had puckered and pinkened. The deep, heavy ones that had been down to the muscle on his side had been grafted with skin from his opposite thigh. In that one area, he was about ten different shades of color, from very dark black to very light.

Cassandra reached out to run her fingers over the skin, feeling the surface, but he watched her face for any hint of hesitation. There was none there. Just curiosity.

"Looks like they patched it?"

"Yes," he cleared his throat. "I have scars on my left thigh where they took the skin grafts from."

"And how did this happen, exactly?"

She shifted back a little, then leaned forward to look more closely at his rib area.

"We were in Iraq on patrol. I was walking along side a Humvee as we cleared a small village. I had just stepped down into a bit of a ditch when the Humvee hit an IED. The blast blew fire out from beneath the vehicle and struck me in the side, knocking me about thirty feet away. My arm was gone immediately, and my side took the brunt of the fire. I was peppered with shrapnel."

She shook her head, her fingers continuing to explore. "I can't imagine the pain."

Her fingers drifted up to the arm and before she could ask, he slipped the prosthetic away from the upper arm stump. He didn't remove the sleeve, but she didn't seem to need that. Her fingers touched the end lightly, feeling its shape and weight before moving on.

As an amputee, you sometimes settled into a casualness with your own body, especially in the company of medical personnel who dealt with injured military. They had usually seen everything during their career. He had no problem walking into a doctor's office and exposing his stub to a room full of interns.

Civilians were another situation entirely. They usually

did double takes, then either stared rudely or turned away and refused to acknowledge you any more.

Roger had never been one to be casual with his appearance. And the relief he felt as Cassandra looked back at him and smiled, her eyes clear of censure or anything negative, was pretty humbling. He'd taken more of a chance with her tonight than any other personal relationship he'd been involved in since his injury.

That was a very long time to be alone.

Roger sighed, appreciating that she was still talking to him and he hadn't apparently grossed her out.

"Honestly, I was pretty lucky," he told her as he replaced the prosthetic. "I had been walking right alongside the vehicle at first. Not sure what made me veer out and down. If I'd still been beside the vehicle I would have lost both my legs and probably bled out. We were a long way from any relief."

Cassandra looked up at him again and smiled, and Roger jerked to attention. He had a beautiful woman with no shirt on right beside him, within reach, and he was rehashing history. Even though his mind was concentrating on other things, his body was still very much focused on her.

He was relieved that she was okay with *him*. That made everything else they had to face minor in comparison.

Cassandra seemed to sense the change in him, and quirked a dark brow. "So, if this is the worst you have to show me I think we'll be okay."

Nodding, he reached out to brush the side of her breast. A shiver worked through her body, and her dark nipples hardened beneath the fabric of her bra.

Cassandra grinned at him. "Keep doing that and I might have to kiss you."

A sense of joyfulness filled him up and he felt like laughing like a child. Instead, he clenched his jaw and mirrored her look, brow quirked. "Oh, really? Maybe if I do this you'll definitely kiss me."

He ran a forefinger around her nipple, through the white cotton. It hardened even more beneath his touch, and he circled it a couple of times before she grabbed his hand and moved it to her other breast. "This one needs attention too," she gasped.

He made the same movement to that nipple as well, and her eyes drifted shut. A moan drifted from her throat and he wondered what she sounded like when she climaxed.

Cassandra shifted her hips, as if the touch transferred to other areas, and Roger wanted to strip her, lay her down and have his way with her.

Shifting to his knees in front of her, he took a moment to adjust himself in his jeans, then cupped her shoulders in his hands. With a gentle nudge, she fell back against the mattress, but her gaze stayed on him.

"You might as well take those jeans off," she told him, voice dry with humor. "I guarantee you're not going to need them."

He grinned, loving that she already had the experience mapped out in her head. "I will in a minute. Right now, it's the only barrier I have strong enough to keep me away from you."

He looked down her body, loving when she arched for him, her curves smoothing. "You have the most delectable body," he whispered. "I have to explore every inch of you."

And he did. As she moaned and sighed, he explored every delicious, scrumptious inch he revealed. When he followed with his lips, she cried out, shifting beneath him. Roger had to stop himself several times because his own hungry body danced on that sharp, hot edge of pleasure. Even the harsh jeans felt good against the head of his cock, and if he wasn't careful he would rub himself raw.

When he sat her up and removed her pretty white bra, though, all coherent thought went out of his head. Her breasts were a bounty, more than his hands could hold, and her nipples were flushed dark with pleasure. When he took one into his mouth, Cassandra gasped and cupped his head to her.

"You're going to kill me, Roger."

Without answering, he drew on the tip of her breast even harder, then shifted to the other side. Damn, she even tasted good here. Gently biting down with his teeth, he let her know how excited he was. But Cassandra apparently loved that edge of pain, her hips shifting more sharply.

Leaving her breasts, Roger moved down her thighs, fingers hooking into the elastic of her panties. He tugged them down slowly, loving that she didn't try to hide herself from him. As he pulled them down the length of her legs, he kissed everything he passed, forcing himself not to look at her most private cleft. He was afraid if he did he would come in his pants.

Drawing in gulping draughts of air, he forced his body to stillness before he allowed himself to look up the length of her.

Oh, God. All thought left his brain as he looked at her. In his wildest imaginings he couldn't have drawn her any more perfect in his mind. From the tops of her soft shoulders, over the bounty of her large breasts, down the length of her tummy to the thatch of dark hair at the apex of her thighs, then her long, long legs, he would not have changed a thing about her. Every piece suited her to a T and fit together to make a masterpiece. She was a heart-stopping vision of beauty, and he was so humbled that she'd chosen him to take to her bed. He would revere her body like no one else ever had.

She watched him, her smart eyes luminous with need and

a little caution. She had body issues as well, she just played them off better than he did.

"You are the moon in my dark night," he told her softly. "You shine with an inner brilliance I've never seen in another human being and I would worship you."

The anxiety eased in her eyes and a tear slipped down her temple. "And I will let you, because I just can't imagine letting you go now."

Roger left the bed and stripped off his jeans and boxers, his cock hard with need. As quickly as he could, he sheathed himself in the only condom he'd had in his wallet. Cassandra's eyes followed him, her eyes widening a little. "Oh my God, you are beautiful. I've never seen anything like you. I want to taste you, Roger."

A bolt of heat arrowed down through his cock.

She started to sit up, but he shook his head. "You have no idea how close to the edge I am right now. You'll have to taste me another time, Cassandra, because if I felt your lips on me I would never last. And I want this night, this morning, to last."

Then, crawling up between her thighs, he gave her the most intimate of nibbles on the inside of her knee. The muscles in her leg quivered as he moved upward, kissing gently here and there, and she began to pant. She knew where he was going, but he wanted to draw out her anticipation. With the tactile fingers of his good hand, he brushed them up along the skin of her thigh, just barely tickling. Her hips shifted and her hands reached for him, but he pressed them to the mattress. Then he explored the soft cloud of hair at the apex of her groin.

Cassandra cried out, her stomach quivering as Roger eased his finger into her wetness.

Oh, damn she was so ready. In the dim light from the hallway, he could see the shine of her arousal on his finger.

Shifting his body, he lay down between her thighs, kissing her soft belly, then moving down.

She tasted like the first swallow of ice water after a hard run, so sweet. He deepened the kiss, lapping at her. Cassandra gave a keening cry, her legs drawing high to allow him deeper access. Roger found her swollen clit with his tongue and, tilting his head, began to suck on the little bundle.

Cassandra cried out and arched, her body contracting in a quick, glorious, orgasm.

Roger loved the sounds she was making. Orgasms could be faked, but not this one. The almost explosive contractions arched her away from him, but he followed her, his mouth strong on her.

His cock tingled and he pulled away, panting. He refused to come like an inexperienced boy, before he'd even entered her. That would be beyond humiliating but he was right on that edge. He had a feeling that as soon as he sank into her creamy heat, he would be *done*.

Clenching his jaw, he rocked back on his heels, lungs billowing. When his heart had settled in his chest, he looked down at Cassandra spread beneath him. When she opened her arms to him, he couldn't deny himself any longer. Moving over her, he looked into her eyes and knew he was a goner. She smiled up at him and lifted her legs, even as she cupped his face in her hands and drew him down. As her lips took his, the head of his cock rested at her entrance and the most amazing feeling of anticipation rolled through him. It was greater than any other feeling he'd ever felt, and as he finally sank into her scalding heat, it only got better, because he knew the pinnacle of pleasure within his reach.

Cassandra Jones had the most amazing body of any woman he'd ever met, and as she tightened her arms around his shoulders, arching up into him, he felt more connected to her than he had any other human being in his life.

"Oh, God, yes..." she sighed, panting as he slid deeply into her.

Condoms tended to mute sensation, but in this one instance he appreciated that fact. It allowed him to feel everything about her he wanted to. The soft cushion of her body, the wet heat of her pussy, the warmth of her arms around him. As she whispered into his ear, Roger shivered and rocked his hips into her. Bracing on his good arm, he lifted enough to look down at her.

Her unique eyes were luminous with pleasure, her plump lips even more plump from his kisses. They spread into a smile as he looked down at her, and she rocked her hips up into his next plunge.

Roger closed his eyes, basking in the feeling. He'd never...

Oh.

She rocked into him again, and reached down to dig her nails into his ass cheeks, pulling him even tighter.

Oh, fuck...

Roger's mind hazed with pleasure and his world narrowed down to the force it took to pump into her body, then draw back. She rocked with him, and started making these delicious sounds deep in her throat, and long drawn out moans. Hearing that she was close again, feeling the rippling of her body, it tugged him along, their pleasure intertwined.

"Harder," she cried out.

Fuck, yes, he could do harder.

Granting her plea was his downfall, though. The heat in his lower back that foretold his release built, and as she arched up to meet his thrusts, her movements frantic as she grabbed at her own release, he was done. With a mighty groan, hips slamming of their own volition, he lost himself in the haze of pleasure that contorted his body. Cassandra cried out with him, her body contracting and releasing in waves as she shattered.

Roger's world spun away, the lancing pleasure focused in his groin, but he was ever conscious of her strong arms holding him to her. His head fell to her heaving chest and he tried to get more oxygen into his lungs. He needed to move off of her, before he smothered her.

Pushing his good arm beneath him, he pushed up, but she stilled his movement with her arms. "Please don't leave yet," she whispered.

And though he was sticky and sweaty and not so fresh anymore, he relaxed into her embrace. His head rested on her breasts and he listened to her heartbeat settle back into a lazy rhythm.

CHAPTER FOUR

For a few minutes, he half dozed there, and it was the most welcoming place he'd ever been in, her lovely arms. Finally, though, he needed to move. The condom needed to be disposed of and his ass was getting cold in the chill of the room.

Levering up, he pressed a kiss to her soft cheek, took a second to kiss the intriguing earring at the top of her ear and moved away, pulling a blanket over top of her luscious body before he headed to the bathroom. He returned within a few minutes and she immediately moved over for him to slide in behind her, spoon style. His hand went to her hip, resting there.

"You wrecked me, Roger Stottsberry," she told him, voice husky. "I don't think I can stand. My legs won't hold me. I've never felt anything like that before."

He smiled at the back of her curly head, till she twisted around to look at him. Once again there were tears in her eyes, and the street smart, cocky personality had faded away.

"I want to be cool and put together, but I just can't do it right now."

He ran his finger down over her shoulder, then down the length of her arm. When he got to her hand, she turned it over and they intertwined fingers.

Roger didn't feel cool either. Everything he'd expected to happen tonight hadn't. "I don't want either one of us to be cool and collected. I think that means we have barriers up between us, and I feel like we're better than that. If this," he tightened his fingers on hers, "has any chance of going anywhere I think we have to be as open as possible. You were very right about that."

She blinked and a tear dripped down her cheek, then another.

"Oh, baby," Roger sighed, turning her fully to face him. He wrapped her in his arms and pulled her tight. Their thighs wrapped around each other and her arms went around his middle to hold him tight.

In this instance, he felt like he needed to reassure her, but he was getting as much out of the intimacy as she was.

"I love it that you turn to me this way," he whispered. "But I feel guilty because you feel so good."

She sputtered out a laugh. "I'm glad to see at least part of you is typical man."

Leaning down, he kissed her slowly, deeply.

"Can I spend the morning in your bed, Cassandra Jones? And maybe the rest of the century?"

Her eyes widened and she clamped her lips shut as if she couldn't contain her joy, then nodded emphatically. As he pulled her into his arms he felt the tears on his shoulder.

~

CASSANDRA EDGED off the bed and padded to the bathroom. Though she kind of hated to do it, she took a shower. It seemed wrong to wash Roger's mark from her body.

But as she did wash she realized how good she felt. Frowning thoughtfully, she ran the soap over her breasts.

Her body felt fantastic, but it was more than that. She felt … lighter in her own skin. Some people would laugh at that and run their gazes over her big, beautiful bod, but she had a feeling Roger wouldn't. He would look into her eyes and smile that perfect male model smile of his. Then tell her how she was his moon. *His moon*. God, that was romantic. Even her jaded ass could admit that.

When she tiptoed into the room, Roger still seemed to be asleep. She crept to her dresser and dug out panties and a bra, then a fresh T-shirt and sleep pants with Dachshunds dancing across the fabric. Roger had closed the drapes when he'd come back to bed, and there was just enough light seeping around the edges to see.

"You are such a beautiful woman," his deep voice rumbled from the darkness. "I know I keep saying it but every time I see you I'm hit with it again."

Cass turned, searching out his form. He'd sat up on the mattress, sheets pooling into folds at his lap. His abs were tight as he arched into a bone-popping stretch, both arms over his head. If Roger were any other man she would think he was posing for her.

But when his gaze connected with hers again, he gave her a little sheepish smile. "I slept really good with you."

"I did too," she told him softly.

And it was the truth. She'd had relationships over the years, but she'd never actually *slept* with a man. That spoke to a trust that she just didn't have; too many of the men she'd known were just aggressive males. But it hadn't even occurred to her to leave the man in her bed last night. She knew Roger had her back, she could trust him to have her back, that was a new feeling for her.

She crossed to the bed and sat down next to him. Immediately, his hand lifted to caress her cheek and he leaned in to give her a good morning kiss. And it wasn't just a peck. It was a *'good morning you luscious, beautiful woman, I want to fuck you'* kiss.

Cass was totally okay with that. As her nipples puckered and her body began to warm, she reached out to touch him. Muscles bulged beneath her fingers, and at his sides the skin quivered, obviously ticklish. She let her fingernails run over the spot a couple of times.

When he pulled away from her mouth, he was grinning. "You're asking for trouble," he warned.

That damn inner devil of hers demanded that she push his limits. Running her fingers over the spot again, a little harder, she quirked a brow at him in a dare.

With a movement quicker than she could follow, he had spun her around till she was face down on the mattress. She felt his fingers in her own sides and she gasped. "Oh, don't you dare! *Roger!*"

In her own bravado, she'd forgotten how very ticklish she was. Roger laid on top of her, full length, his hands beneath her arm pits. Cass gasped and wiggled, but that only made Roger's fingers move into her skin. She stilled, quivering, laughing.

"I'm not moving," he told her softly, kissing her at the nape of her neck. "I'm just exploring, like you were, right?"

"Right," she gasped, trying not to break into giggles.

Roger's hands glided down her sides, and she was surprised that she could barely tell the difference between his two hands. They moved exactly the same, the only difference was, the prosthetic skin caught on the fabric of her T, dragging it a little.

Then she lost her train of thought because he tugged the T-shirt up her back.

Cass tried not to wince in embarrassment, but it was

really hard. Her weight had been an issue for such a long time. She'd taught herself over the years to be carefree, like it didn't hurt at all what people said or did. But in times like these, when her body was under such intense scrutiny, all those insecurities flooded back. Yes, in the past couple of years she'd learned to eat better and exercise more, but the weight she'd lost didn't seem to matter right this second.

Roger ran a finger down the center of her spine, brushing the shirt up and out of his way. Then his hand swept out to cup her side, in almost the same area she'd been tickling him.

Her skin crept away from his touch, quivering, and he chuckled deeply as she squirmed beneath his weight. "Oh, baby, you are just a wonder. I think you're as ticklish as I am right here. That wasn't very smart, daring me, was it? It left you very vulnerable."

She gasped as he ran the lightest of touches over the spot again. "No," she gasped, voice high. "I'm sorry, Roger. I won't do it again. That was a bad move on my part."

"Mm," he murmured. Then he shifted and his lower hips flexed into her.

Cass gasped for a completely different reason. She had a startling flashback of that hard length moving inside her last night, and a frisson of need sliced through her. Her hips shifted on the mattress.

Roger stilled above her. "Damn woman. One little move and you've got me rock hard. It's this perfect damn ass, pushing up into me. You know I'm going to have to fuck you like this, soon."

"Why not now?" she asked, doing a little circular grind.

"Because I only had one condom with me, damn it. And we used it last night."

"There's a strip of condoms in the top drawer of the dresser behind you," she whispered.

Roger froze for a moment, and she almost thought she

could feel the pulse tighten his dick even further, before he pushed off of her. She heard him yank open the drawer and go rifling through her panties, then the unmistakable sound of a foil wrapper being ripped open. She glanced over her shoulder and had to draw in a breath.

Roger Stottsberry had the nicest dick she'd ever seen. Last night he'd been kind of hidden, but this morning he stood proudly before her, ready. He glanced at her lying on the bed and something flared in his eyes before he moved behind her. Cass felt him grip the sides of her sleep pants and drag them down and off her feet. Then his strong hands spanned over her ass cheeks, measuring, feeling, spreading. A finger wedged between her thighs, then delved into her heat. Cass arched as he found her slickness and he began to tease her. Burying her face into the comforter, she clutched the fabric in her fists as her hips began to move. She spread her thighs so that he could reach her more easily.

It was incredible, the way he touched her. Not too light, not too fast. He'd been with enough women to know what brought them pleasure. And though she hadn't been looking for sex five minutes ago, he brought it to her hard. She moaned as the first hard clutch of orgasm shuddered through her, stealing her breath, arching her up off the bed. And just as she was regaining her equilibrium, he propped her hips up a couple of inches and slid into her.

This position felt very different than missionary, and they both cried out as Roger settled into a deep, hard, gliding rhythm, driving toward release. There was no hesitation this time, just a demanding need for pleasure. He made sure that she was taken care of, though, too. Kissing her on the back of the neck, squeezing her hips and her breasts. But it was his words that did her in. Roger told her how perfect she was, and what a blessing it was that he had met her, and that he never wanted to let her go.

That was the one that pushed her over the edge, screaming out to the room in time with his thrusts. Her pleasure was a wild thing, trying to buck him off. And as he found his own release, the wildness consumed him as well. He gasped her name into the room, his weight collapsing on top of her.

Cass didn't say anything, just turned her head to the side so that she could breathe. Aftershocks rippled through her, and she could feel how wet she was. That was new. Roger had gotten her *really* excited, she thought with a chuckle.

"I just took a shower, damn it," Cassandra groused as she lay beside him, trying to catch her breath.

Roger chuckled. "I'm sorry, baby. Well, no, I'm not."

Laughing deep in his throat he rolled away from her light pinch, then turned back to look at her. Her hair was crazy and her skin make-up free, but he seemed to drink her up with his eyes. She still wore the silly wiener dog T-shirt, but no pants or undies. He'd kind of ripped those off of her.

"It's your fault anyway." He waved at her shirt. "Obviously, you were thinking of my dick when you got up."

She looked down at her breasts, and the grinning dog, then howled with laughter. Roger laughed with her, and she loved that he teased her like this. As soon as they were done making love, some tension had crept between them, but they weren't going to let it take hold.

He gave her a smack on her bare ass. "Get cleaned up and let's get out of here. I'm hungry."

CHAPTER FIVE

IT WAS ONLY LATER, driving through the snow-laden streets, that they remembered that it was Christmas Day. They drove, carefully, through the streets, looking for a restaurant or grocery store but nothing was open other than a few gas stations.

"Well," Roger said finally. "Eventually the movie theaters will open, right? There are new releases today. We just have to wait until then."

Cass snorted and shrugged. "Sure. I don't have anywhere to be."

So, they drove through the snowy morning and just talked. Cass told him about growing up on the streets in Denver, her mother perpetually addicted to something. When she'd finally overdosed for the last time, leaving them alone, it had been a blessing in disguise, because it had gotten them off the street for good. The orphanage they'd been sent to hadn't been luxurious by any means, but to two young children who had never known a bed or clean clothing, it had been a wonder. The staff had tried to keep Andre and her together, and it had worked for the most part. They'd stayed there for several years until Cass had been old enough to get out on her own.

It had been a tough few years, but she'd done the best she could with what they'd had.

"You're amazing," Roger told her, glancing at her from the driver's seat. "Not everyone would have stepped up like that. You did a remarkable thing, petitioning the state to take in your brother like that. I can only imagine how hard it was."

Tears suddenly obscured her vision and she had to turn to look out the window. She had worked her ass off, going to school and working and taking care of Andre, making sure he was doing everything he was supposed to be doing. But had anyone recognized that? No. They'd only bitched when she'd screwed something up.

"Thank you," she whispered. "I learned a huge amount in those few years Andre and I lived together. We both did. And we both knew what we *didn't* want, that's why he entered the military."

She glanced at him. "Even when he was a little bugger, he wanted to be an Army man. So, that's what I pushed him to do. He graduated high school and enlisted the same week. He left for basic within a few months. It was a couple of years but it seems like just a little while later he was deployed to Afghanistan and they were contacting me to let me know there'd been an 'unfortunate accident'."

Roger reached over and she was amazed at the amount of comfort she could feel radiating through his prosthetic hand.

"I'm sorry, Cassandra. Friendly fire accidents don't happen often, but when they do they affect entire bases, entire companies. I'm sorry."

She shrugged, running her fingernails over the smooth outer finish. "It was better he died over there than on the streets here. It's so hard for young black men to reach for anything. He was doing what he'd dared to reach for."

"Just like you are."

Smiling, she allowed him to guide the conversation to happier things. "Yes, I am. I used his death benefit to finish putting myself through school and move away from the Five Points."

Roger winced. He was probably very aware of what the Five Points were. The urban area northeast of the city center was low income, high crime. Definitely one of the most dangerous areas in Denver. The fact that she'd found the means to get out of the area spoke to her determination as a strong woman. She was proud of herself for that. It would have been so much easier to fall into the patterns of her mother, stealing and whoring herself out for the drugs she used.

Cass wasn't proud of where she'd grown up, but she was proud of what she'd accomplished. It had taken her four years to get through graphic design school, but she'd relished the schooling. It had challenged her, and given her a purpose. It had given her something to focus on other than the fact that she was so very alone in the world.

In fact, there was a very real possibility that she was with Roger because she was lonely. She winced, hating that she'd even thought that. Roger was more to her than just a pacifier. He was quickly becoming more to her than anything else in the world.

"Oh, yes," he hissed. They had just passed beneath an interstate underpass and found a big, brightly lit, expansive travel station. Semis lined one side of the parking lot and cars the other. People were moving around and it looked like business as usual. Actually, it was probably a little more busy than normal because it was the *only* thing open at the moment.

Roger parked the car and took her hand as she met him at the front of the Jeep.

"I bet we can find breakfast, lunch, and a midnight snack here."

She waved a hand at one of the neon signs, bright even in the daylight. "As well as a twenty-four hour masseuse slash dentist."

Shaking their heads, they laughed together and started walking toward the gas station. It was huge inside, and obviously catered to a very diverse clientele. There were drink coolers and food coolers, a well as several hot counter ovens with 'roller' food. Ewww...

Before she moved from the doorway, Roger gripped her hand in his own. "Not so fast, baby."

He glanced at the top of the entryway. There, hanging from the ceiling on a thin fishing line, was a bunch of plastic mistletoe.

Cass looked at him incredulously, trying to gather her thoughts. A woman stomped around them, aggravated at being moved off her trajectory.

"You don't seriously expect me to stand here and kiss you," she told him.

He gave her a lopsided smile and held his hand out to her. "Are you embarrassed to kiss me in public? I know I'm a beat up old Marine but I didn't think you'd hold it against me."

Huffing out a breath, Cass shook her head. "Beat up old Marine my ass," she muttered and leaned up for a kiss.

Roger met her halfway, but when she would have drawn back, his arms tightened around her. The kiss deepened. Cass gasped as he lowered her into a theatrical dip, sending her tummy into free-fall, then lifted her back up as if she were a skinny little bitch. She stared into his dark eyes, dazed.

Grinning, Roger reached out to straighten the lapels of her coat as the few people gathered around them clapped.

With a huff, Cass turned away, shaking her head. But she

had to admit she was secretly thrilled with the little show. "You're a madman," she hissed. "You and your mistletoe mischief."

Laughing out loud, Roger cupped her ass in his hand and squeezed. Before she could turn around to smack him, he had disappeared.

They went their separate ways to find food, but most of the fare they found was pretty scary. There were all the gray sandwiches with mystery meat she could choose from...um, no.

The Subway counter was open, so she headed in that direction. Roger had the same idea, because he met her halfway there. As natural as breathing, their hands reached toward each other and clasped. It was sheer lunacy that he'd completely obliterated her natural reserve in less than twenty-four hours.

Cass ran her fingers over his as they stopped in line. Behind the counter a frazzled woman wrapped sandwiches for waiting customers.

Cass and Roger waited patiently. They moved forward slowly, till they got to the register. Roger smiled at the woman to try to set her at ease, but it wasn't until she caught sight of his prosthetic hand that she actually looked up into his eyes. "Can I help you?"

He nodded and leaned in toward her, turning on the charm. "I know you're so busy. I appreciate you being here, though. I thought we were going to starve to death."

The woman flushed under the attention, as she tucked some flyaway hair behind her ears. "What can I get you?"

Roger gave her his order, then motioned for Cass to give hers. Moving quickly and efficiently, the woman rang them up then made their sandwiches. Roger smiled at her and Cass thought he might have even tossed in a wink, but she was in the wrong position to see for sure. She was reminded of a saying. Something about judging the character of others by how they treat those that can do nothing for them. Yes, the lady was making them a sandwich, but he didn't have to be nice to her to get it. That was just the kind of guy Roger was.

As they took their sandwiches he wished the woman a very merry Christmas. She smiled. "Thank you. I will. Merry Christmas to you and your wife as well."

Cassandra jerked in her boots. Wife? The thought sent a little thrill through her, but she tamped it down. The thought of marriage had never ever entered her mind, not with any man.

Roger just smiled, though, like he heard it every day and moved deeper into the store. They wandered the aisles and talked about the things they saw; snacks, books, movies. The travel plaza catered to a large truck driver clientele, so there was actually a very large selection of just miscellaneous stuff.

Then they came to the Christmas tree. Obviously, it was meant for the truckers who hadn't had a chance to shop for the loved ones in their lives before they headed home. Beneath the tree were stacks of wrapped presents, with small, white removable tags suggesting who they could go to. Male gift, female gift, male child eight to ten. It was actually an ingenious, convenient little set up. The truckers were usually men away from their families and this gave them an opportunity to not look like they sucked when they came home empty handed.

Roger's mouth split in a grin as he looked from the tree back to her. "If I had known I was going to have this much fun with you, I'd have bought you a Christmas present before the date. Want to shop here? Now?"

Cass barked out a laugh, but the suggestion kind of appealed to her as well. There was an intriguing playfulness in the thought of getting a completely random gift.

"Let's do it!"

She started sorting through the packages, looking for one for a male. The prices on the tags ranged from a few dollars to several hundred dollars. She found a long, thin one, and discarded it. Then she found a tall, rectangular, heavy one. It had a tag for a male, but was wrapped in glittery pink paper. Giggling, she cradled the box to her chest. "Okay, I have mine."

Roger looked at the paper and narrowed his eyes at her in a skeptical look. "Really?"

Turning to the tree, he started sorting through the packages. Within a few minutes, he found a long tubular package. It was at least two feet long and was actually wrapped pretty nicely, in silver paper and a red bow.

Cassandra's stomach clenched at the thought of getting a present, and it was a stupid reaction. But since her brother had been gone, she hadn't had enough of a connection to anyone to get more than generic gifts from the girls at the office when they did the holiday exchange.

How sad was that?

They got in line to pay and she was surprised at the amount that rang up for Roger's gift.

"That's too expensive," she hissed behind him, poking him in the ribs.

He shushed her and blocked her with his broad shoulder.

"No, it's *snot*," he whispered.

She looked at him sharply, trying to decide if she'd heard what she thought she did. His eyes glinted with suppressed laughter and she shook her head at him.

"Why are all men so gross?"

Before she could challenge him again, he swiped his card and the transaction was completed. Cass huffed as she rang up her own items, then followed him back out to the Jeep. Roger started the car and bumped up the heat, but then he turned in his seat. "Do you want to eat or open our gifts first?"

Excitement bubbled up inside her and she allowed herself to grin at him. "Presents."

With a single nod, he handed her the pretty wrapped package. "You first."

She shook her head adamantly. "Nope. You first. I want to draw my excitement out a little more."

Laughing, Roger nodded. Holding the package down against the center console with his prosthetic, he started peeling back the paper with his other hand. Cass turned in her seat, leaning forward to see what was revealed. Roger seemed to be deliberately going slow, and making her wonder. When he finally pulled back the package, he had a surprised look on his face.

"Well, I'll be darned…"

Inside the pretty pink wrapping paper was a fairly comprehensive looking micro tool set. Roger popped open the lid. "You know, this is the size I use on one of the adjustments on my elbow joint."

Though it was covered with the jacket, he indicated the inside of his right elbow.

"This is a surprisingly appropriate gift." Leaning forward, he coaxed her in for a kiss. Cass met him halfway. She was more than happy to, actually. "Thank you for my gift, baby. I love it. I know you put a lot of time into picking it out and wrapping it just right."

They laughed together at the ridiculousness of the statement. He nodded his head at the brightly wrapped package at her feet.

"Your turn."

Cass lifted the gift and began to peel the paper, trying not to tear it.

"Are you actually going to use that paper again?"

She paused and looked at what she was doing, shook her head and began to tear the paper haphazardly. It was a tube, with no indication of what was inside. The end of the tube popped off easily and she began pulling out tissue paper.

And more tissue paper. And more.

"What the hell?" she muttered.

Finally, a small, hard, wrapped box fell into her hand when she upended the tube and gave it a good shake. It was wrapped in the same silver paper. Cass stared at it for several long seconds before she started unwrapping again. This time she revealed a small chocolate box that said *Kentucky Bourbon Balls* across the top. She gave Roger a critical look.

"If you spent that much money for chocolate I'm going to march right back in there and get your money back."

Roger was grinning, though, as if he knew what was in the package. Cass opened the box and pulled out another wad of tissue paper. She began unraveling it. Finally, a shining gold ring was revealed. Cass gasped as the stone caught the light. It looked like a real diamond. And the gold looked real, too.

Beside her, Roger snorted.

"Well, if that isn't a message I don't know what is," he murmured.

Cass began to shake as he took the ring from her trembling fingers. Her gaze lifted to his in spite of the fear in her heart.

There was a calm smile on his incredibly handsome face. He took her left hand in his own. "Cassandra Jones, I've had an unbelievable night and day with you. Going on a blind date with you was the best thing I've done in a very, *very* long time. Would you consider this ring a promise to invest in exploring this relationship further? We'll call it a pre-engagement ring."

Cass sniffed, trying not to bawl in front of him, but it was hard. He slipped the ring onto her left ring finger and she gasped. It fit as if it had been made for her.

A tear rolled down her cheek to drop onto their clasped hands. Tugging her toward him, Roger kissed away her tears. Then he kissed her lips.

Cass couldn't breathe. There were so many emotions raging in her body. She had no idea what to say or do. She couldn't even get a full breath.

"If you don't at least nod or say yes," Roger said, voice deep, "you're going to break my heart."

Then she could hear the anxiety in his own trembling voice. This wasn't easy for him either.

"*Yes,*" she told him firmly, taking in a huge gulp of air. She needed to tell him what she felt. "You scare the bejeezus out of me but I definitely want to explore this *thing* between us. You have made me feel more in the past twenty-four hours than I've felt in the past four years. No, let me change that. You've made me feel more in the past twenty-four hours than I ever have in my *life*. I want to live like this with you, discovering everything about you, loving you."

His eyes gleamed with moisture and she blinked to clear her vision. She couldn't imagine anyone being this emotional over *her*. The girl with nothing.

Roger leaned in and rested his wet cheek against her own, then he kissed her. He tasted spectacular, even more so now that she knew this was *her* man.

Damn that sounded so strange. That plastic mistletoe mischief had actually worked…

EPILOGUE

ROGER LOOKED at what he held in his hand and felt an elemental shift in the very core of his being. Cassandra was more woman than he'd ever met before, and he was fascinated bc everything she did. They'd been together for days now, every spare hour they could get together, but he had no desire to leave. Ever.

That was a very strange feeling for him. Normally, after a few hours, he needed to escape whatever company he was with. Even his buddies from work could wear on his nerves eventually, but not Cassandra. Every expression on her face, every movement of her body, every word out of her mouth was fascinating and precious to him.

And now he was counting down minutes until she called. He had to work later tonight, but he would spend the evening hours with her.

Excitement burrowed through him. She was late calling, and he was anxious as hell to get over there to be with her.

Moving around the apartment, he picked up a few clothes, tossing them into the laundry basket. There were a few dishes he loaded into the washer. All busywork he'd put off while he'd been absorbed in her.

When the text lit up his phone that she was leaving work, he gathered his things and walked out the door.

He would be starting the rest of his life *tonight*.

CASS LOOKED OUT THE WINDOW, wondering if she had time to hop into the shower before Roger got there for dinner. An unexpected snafu at work had derailed her regular escape time, and she hoped he was okay with eating quickie spaghetti, salad and garlic bread. They hadn't talked about Italian food yet.

Seems like they'd talked about everything else *but* that.

This week had been joyous to her, and terrifying. So far, Roger had been everything she'd hoped for and more. She looked down at the ring on her finger, still shocked to see it there. He hadn't shown any regret at giving her the promise ring. In fact, he'd started running his thumb over it as often as possible, as if to remind himself that it was real as well.

Cass didn't know if the ring was actually worth anything —hell, it could be glass for all she knew—but she didn't care. The sentimental value was more important than anything. Other than the pictures of her brother, the ring had become the thing she prized most in her life.

No, that wasn't right. The ring was a prized possession but Roger had become the *most* important thing in her life.

Inwardly, she cringed, but that was how it felt in her bones. He belonged with her. Period. If this was some kind of psychotic break or schizophrenic episode, she hoped they never found a cure. Because her crazy and Roger's crazy fit perfectly.

Pouring a little salt into the pot of boiling water, she got everything ready to cook when Roger walked in the door. The bread was warming in the oven and the noodles were on the counter, ready to be dropped into the water. The salad was made and ready to go.

She looked up at the clock. Almost six-thirty. Roger had to leave for the graveyard shift at LNF at ten-thirty. They would have four hours together tonight but he was off the next day.

It freaked her out how easy it had been to fall into a schedule this week. As soon as she left work, Roger came over for dinner and cuddling before he had to leave for work. Then, in the mornings, he would bring her coffee from McDonalds before he headed to his own apartment to sleep.

They'd seen each other every day since Christmas, and it wasn't enough.

Roger seemed to feel the same way. They'd started texting each other, and some of the conversations were obnoxiously sweet. A couple of times, Cass had looked down at the phone in her hand and shaken her head at what she'd written. It didn't make sense. It was so out of character for her.

But it made her happy. And it felt right.

She'd also had to upgrade the small text message plan for her cell phone.

Brenda was over the moon that her matchmaking had worked, and tended to gloat when she caught Cass mooning over something Roger did or said. Cass let her, because she was thankful. It would probably get irritating eventually, but for now she'd let Brenda have her glory.

Tomorrow night she and Roger had plans to meet the guys and their significant others at the Frog Dog. She was being reintroduced to the group as Roger's *significant other*. Her stomach bottomed out at the thought. Even though she'd met them before, she hadn't expected to ever meet them again.

Shit was getting real.

Her quiet life was expanding. Fast.

And though there was some lingering fear in her heart, she would try to be strong, a partner to complement Roger.

What the hell did she do?

There was a tap on her door and she crossed the apartment to answer it. Damn. Would this fluttery feeling in her stomach ever go away?

When she opened the door, she was struck dumb, just looking at him. Roger stood on the other side, of course, heavy coat bundled around him, looking like a damn GQ model. He wore a black skullcap low over his forehead and ears, and his broad mouth was spread in a smile. As soon as he saw her he pulled her in for a hello kiss. Cass reached up to cup his neck, finally able to breathe now that she was in his arms.

When they were apart, anxiety plagued her. In her mind, nothing was as good as she thought. They weren't in love, and they weren't so drawn to each other that they couldn't be apart. Surely she hadn't allowed herself to become one of those simpering women that doted on their men...

Then he walked into her line of sight and all of the poles aligned again. Those feelings that she scoffed at during the light of day rebounded back, and she was so in love with him that she couldn't breathe. And he was, too.

Even now as he cupped her cheek and ran his hand down her body, she could feel the need in him.

"I missed you, baby."

Cass shivered at his words. "I missed you, too."

He pulled her in against him. She gave a little cry as he lifted her up to move her inside the jamb, then he kicked the door shut behind them.

"I've been thinking about you all day and I woke up hard and aching, and craving you."

Arousal curled through her lower body and it was all she could do to keep her feet. Just those few words totally annihilated what she'd planned for the night. But that was okay. Reaching up, she began to unbutton her blouse, but he stayed her hand.

"Not yet, baby. I want to talk to you for a minute."

He tugged her to the couch and sat her down into the cushion, then he angled toward her. Cass tried not to be worried, but something about his tone seemed awfully serious.

"What's wrong?"

Roger cleared his throat and glanced out over the room, as if he needed time avoiding her scrutiny. "You know I love you," he started.

The bottom fell out of her stomach. Dread grabbed her heart with sharp fingers and her breath stalled in her lungs.

No, please no... she would never recover from him leaving her.

"It's about us getting together this weekend with the guys."

Ok, maybe this wasn't what she thought.

"I don't have to go," she told him quickly, praying that that was what the issue was.

He shook his head, pocketing the skull cap. "No, it's not that."

Distracted, he stood up to take his coat off, then dropped cap and coat to the adjoining chair, but he didn't sit down again. Instead, turning to her, he knelt down on one knee in front of her.

"Cassandra, my love, I felt cheated when that ring fell out of that tissue paper. I've been replaying it in my mind and I don't want us," he made a motion with his prosthetic hand, "to be connected because of chance. I want us to be together because we have to be, we *need* to be, and because we can't imagine *not* being together. I know I can't. You've become as important to me as my right arm, so to speak." He grinned at her, white teeth flashing. "I can't imagine walking through life without you by my side. So, this weekend when I take you to Frog Dog, I don't want to introduce you as my girlfriend..."

He paused, his gaze connecting with hers.

"I want to introduce you as my beautiful fiancée."

With his good hand he reached into his pant pocket and withdrew a box. Flipping the lid open, he presented it to her.

Black spots swirled in her vision when she looked down at the gleaming ring sitting in a blue velvet cushion.

No way. He didn't...

Oh, yes, he did.

Cass couldn't control her quaking hands or her tearing eyes. Luckily, Roger was handy for stuff like that. He reached out and gripped her left wrist with his prosthetic, drawing the arm closer to him. With the other hand, he slipped the gleaming white platinum ring with the huge diamond onto her finger, right next to the other one.

Cass was speechless, and so in love. There were no words to describe the depth of her love for the man in front of her, or the rightness of it. She'd never seen a relationship like it before in her life, so it had caught her totally off guard.

As he fit the ring to her finger, she folded her hand over his. "I," she had to pause to clear her tight throat, "I would be so incredibly *proud* and humble to be introduced as your fiancée. Roger, you are every dream I never knew I could have."

Tears slipped down her cheeks, but she blamed it on Roger. The man stirred her emotions like she'd never known and could make her cry at the drop of a hat. She had no defense against him, and she didn't want one.

He laughed deeply and wrapped her in his arms. They

leaned back against the couch and he kissed her like he was a parched man.

Cass felt the same desperate need to be as close to him as possible.

Roger peppered kisses across her cheeks and down her neck. "I want you to move in with me. I know it's sudden, but I want to be with you every single moment I can."

That didn't sound bad at all to Cass. "Okay. I'll start packing tomorrow."

He pulled back to grin down at her. "Really? Just like that?"

She nodded once. "Yes. Just like that. You are my life now, Roger Stottsberry. I go where you go."

"I love you more than anything, Cassandra. I will give you a good life. I'll make you happy," he promised.

She shook her head at him. "You already have, you wonderful man. I could die tomorrow and I would have lived a life I'd never begun to hope for. Thank you."

ROGER UNDRESSED her then and there, leaving her wearing only the rings. They glinted in the light as she cupped his cheek, and he could feel the love radiating from her. Hell, he could *see* the love radiating from her in every touch of her hands.

The woman had bowled him over with her spirit and tenacity and acceptance.

He would live his life making hers the very best he possibly could.

GABE

CHAPTER ONE

TWO DAYS AFTER CHRISTMAS

As HE LEFT the Lost and Found office, Gabe wracked his brain, trying to puzzle out what he could get Julie. It was kind of difficult to come up with just the right thing. They were at a place in their lives where if they wanted or needed something, they could just go out and buy it. Maybe he could get her some fabric for the quilting she'd taken up recently. No, he wouldn't have any idea of what kind to get her or what color or anything.

The creative direction had some potential, though. Maybe he would go to a craft store and wander around. Perhaps inspiration would strike.

Actually implementing the plan, though, was a little harder to do. When he parked his truck in the Jo-Ann's Fabrics store parking lot, he was suddenly overcome with a sense of dread. The lot wasn't full, by any means, but something held him immobile. Then Gabe remembered Duncan's words about finding direction when he got stressed. He could do this. He had direction. *Julie*. Julie deserved a great Christmas and he was going to make it happen.

He slipped out of the truck and headed toward the door,

determination strengthening his steps. The pain in his right leg from the gunshot wound disappeared and he forgot about his worries as he focused on Julie. She was the most important part of his day, his life, his world, and he needed to honor her somehow.

That was all well and good until he walked into the huge store. Colors, smells, and bright lights bombarded his senses and he had to pause inside the automatic doors. Then, conscious of people coming in behind him, he stepped to the side of the door. Even with the sunglasses still shading his eyes, he felt under attack. Sensory overload was a very real thing. Moving instinctively, he headed toward a less populated area of the store and started wandering the aisles.

Gabe considered himself a worldly man, but he saw so many items in this store that he had no idea what they were for or how anyone would use them, that he almost felt like his brain would explode. Julie loved going shopping at Jo-Ann's, he knew that, he'd seen the bags in the recycling tub. But what she bought here was a complete mystery to him—hmph, some investigator he was.

"Can I help you?"

Gabe looked down at the little woman that had appeared at his side and cursed to himself. What a great SEAL he was, being snuck up on by a little grandma type. His only excuse was that he was too wrapped up in being overwhelmed. "I, uh, don't know. I'm looking for a Christmas present, but I'm not sure what I should get."

The woman, Kate her name tag read, nodded as if she'd heard the words before and pushed her glasses up on her nose. "Is this for your wife or girlfriend?"

He almost said wife, then wondered why he didn't. "Wife."

"You're in the flower arranging section. Is that what she likes to do?"

He glanced around at the strange green foam pieces and

spools of wire. So that's what this stuff was for. "No. She likes to quilt."

The woman smiled at him. "Ah, perfect! Follow me."

Gabe followed her through the brightly lit store, dodging people and carts and yelling kids. He kept telling himself that this was for Julie. She needed to know how special she was to him. He needed to *show* her how special. He tried to tell her as much as he could, but even that got lost in translation sometimes. And their schedules didn't help either. Half the time they were on opposite schedules, passing in the hallway or *maybe* having a meal together, usually breakfast.

The woman led him to rows upon rows of fabrics, then a row beyond to more strange looking items.

"I need to ask you a few things. Is she a beginning quilter or has she been doing this a while?"

Gabe frowned. "Well, she said she learned it from her grandmother but she's just taken it up again recently since we moved here."

"Does she do everything by hand or does she use a machine?"

The woman held a hand out to an oddly shaped white machine.

"We don't have one of those in the apartment, I know that much."

Finally, something he was sure about.

"Well, these are a little pricey but if you're looking for something amazing this would be a very nice gift. Once she puts the pieces of fabric together to make the quilt top, they have to be quilted onto batting and the backing. This machine can handle all of that."

Gabe leaned down to look at the machine, and the little display.

The woman pointed out several buttons and levers. "She can do all of her piecing on this machine and do the quilting, too, as long as the quilt isn't too large. Many times, quilters have to send their quilts out to be quilted, but she wouldn't have to do that with this machine."

Gabe looked at the price tag, and it was a little expensive —about the cost of a nice Glock... or two—but Julie was worth it. "I'll take that. Definitely. What else can I get her?"

The woman smiled and walked him along the aisle, pointing things out. Gabe thought Julie might have a rotary cutting tool, it looked vaguely familiar, but he got her another one anyway. As well as pins with colorful heads; wide, see through rulers, and special mats that she could cut things on. Kate assured him that even if she had these items already, they'd be welcome gifts because they were all extremely useful for a quilter. The saleswoman disappeared at one point to go get him a cart, and Gabe was amazed at the amount of stuff that they piled into it. He looked at the gray-haired woman. "Thank you for helping me. I had no idea what to get her."

She rested a hand on the edge of the cart and gave him a smile. "Yeah, you had that look about you. We have a lot of military guys come in here looking for something special, but they have no idea what."

Gabe chuckled, for the first time feeling like he was kind of normal. "How did you know I was military?"

Kate gave him a look over the top of her glasses, her laughter gone. "You have the look of a man hurting and lost, even with the dark glasses on. I saw you when you came in the store and knew I needed to talk to you," she smiled softly. "You remind me of my son Charles. He was a Marine and loved his wife like there was no tomorrow, but he had the same kind of look to him for a long time. It wasn't until my grandbaby was hit riding her bicycle that he came around and started being there for them. Little Dahlia recovered and after that he was so much more... *present* in every way. He'd been a walking ghost for a couple of years when he came back from the war, but Dahlia's accident woke him up finally."

Gabe swallowed, struck by the ghost analogy. Yeah, that's what he'd felt like for a long time, since he'd come out to Colorado. He felt ephemeral and insignificant. Unless he was with Julie. Maybe it was because she'd been there for so long, through all of his transitions, shifts and transformations from one life to another. She had been his one guiding star, his true North.

He held a hand out to Kate. "I can't thank you enough for everything that you've done. I'm very glad that your son came back to his family."

The woman smiled again and nodded her head. "He just needed a little direction."

Gabe walked away from her feeling more solid in his mind than he had in a long time. As he was walking toward the cash registers at the front of the store, something caught his attention. It was a plaque, about two feet by two feet square sitting on an end cap display. 'Man, just like a compass needle, will wobble before finding his true North. You are my true North.'

The sense of rightness that settled into him was significant. He didn't generally believe in coincidences, but between talking to Kate and seeing the sign, he felt like he was meant to be there. Grabbing the sign, he set it in the cart as well, then chose a line to check out.

Now how the *hell* was he going to wrap all this stuff?

CHAPTER TWO

JULIE DIDN'T KNOW what to think when she pulled up to the apartment. Even though it was seven fifteen in the morning a couple of days *after* Christmas, there were new Christmas lights strung along the balcony of their apartment and down the railing of the stairway. She slowed as she realized there was even a simple wreath on her door. She had decorated the inside of the apartment, but she hadn't done any of this.

She opened the door carefully, wondering if she needed to be on the lookout for elves. Nope, no elves, just a bangin' hot former Navy SEAL sitting on the couch in his skivvies, scrubbing his face with his hands like he'd just woken up. Twelve hours of a thankless shift, sore back, and aching feet just faded away in a heartbeat.

"Hello," she said softly. "This is a nice surprise."

Gabe smiled, hopped up from the couch and crossed the room to her. Julie dropped her things to the floor and leaned up to meet his kiss. Rather than one of the little pecks he'd been giving her recently, he gave her a bone-melting, lingering *kiss*.

"Now *that's* how it's supposed to be done," she smiled.

Gabe grinned at her, his dark eyes heavy-lidded with sleep. "Welcome home," he rumbled.

Julie blinked, wondering what had brought on the change. Damn, was this all because of Duncan's little admonishment to be more engaged?

Gabe turned and tugged her to the couch. "Have a seat. I know you have to be tired."

She was, but not so much that she wouldn't sit with him. "I'm surprised to see you up," she admitted.

"Well, I was excited," he told her, grinning sheepishly.

Uh oh...

"Why are you excited?"

He held up his hands. "It's our first Christmas together, and I realized that in the rush of moving out here and getting settled, we kind of lost sight of *us*. I need to get my head on straight and focus on what's really important."

Her eyes turned misty and she leaned forward to give him a short kiss. "I admit I've been a little distracted, too. The new job at the VA has taken some getting used to. And going from a regular office hours kind of nursing job to nights and swing shift with no seniority is hard. Christmas was a just blip on my radar."

"Yeah, I'm in the same boat. And I have to be honest, I feel some heavy duty guilt for leaving the Teams."

She cocked her head. "Why? You were injured. There wasn't anything you could do about that."

He shrugged and rubbed a hand over his bristled jaw. "I know that in my head, but in my heart I worry that someone is going to get hurt because I'm not there. I was damn good at my job."

She smiled at him, nodding. "I know. Butter was always full of stories about you. Remember?"

His smiled turned sad as he remembered his lost friend, but he nodded. "Yeah, I remember. I think we had just as many stories about him, though. We were a really good team."

Leaning close, she rubbed his back, wishing that he could let go of his worries. "I love that you're talking to me like this. You have a tendency to clam up and disappear. If I don't watch you sometimes, you just walk away."

Wincing, he leaned into her shoulder. "I'm sorry I do that. Sometimes I just get wrapped up in my head and I don't think about anything else. Or something makes me feel panicky. I talked to Duncan today and he gave me some ideas about getting on track and staying focused. But I want you to know that *you* are my priority. I love you. I really, really do. I can't imagine where I would be without you."

The tears were back. "I love you, too, Gabe, and whatever you need us to do to keep straight, we'll do."

He gave her a rueful smile. "I have a feeling that if we've made it through this year we'll make it through *anything*."

Julie laughed, knowing he was exactly right.

"So," he said, smacking his knees with his hands and pushing up from the couch to walk over to the little Christmas tree. "To that end, I got you some things. I know we had talked about waiting till this weekend, but I don't think I can wait. I want to see your face when you open these."

Julie laughed as he drew a laundry basket full of hand-wrapped gifts out from behind the tree. There was one big box, then several other oddly shaped— and even more oddly wrapped— packages. In spite of herself, excitement surged through her. Hopping up, she ran to the bedroom to get the purple canvas Thirty-One bag full of his presents. She tore off her dirty scrubs and pulled on a long sleep shirt, then headed back out to the living room.

Though she was tired, sharing this experience with him

was much more important than sleep. And the fact that *Gabe* had initiated their celebration had her heart soaring.

As they alternated opening gifts, she felt that connection strengthening, reaffirming itself between them. Gabe's lean face expressed joy and humble pride as he opened his last gift, a shadow box for the Silver Star he had received 'for valor during intense urban fighting' he'd been part of in Ramadi. That's what the presidential letter said, anyway. Gabe hadn't told her what he had done because it was still classified, but she'd seen footage on the news. It had been a devastating series of conflicts, and she was amazed he'd come home at all.

"I thought that since you were retired now," she said softly, "you wouldn't mind displaying it. If I'm wrong, we can put it in the closet until you're ready."

He shook his head, eyes unfocused and lost to memories. Deliberately, she reached out to rest her hand on his thigh, and he jerked, his gaze finding hers. He blinked a couple of times, his focus sharpening. "I would... I do want to display it. Thank you, Julie."

Gathering her in his arms, he wrapped himself tightly around her, sharing strength. Julie knew that he needed this more than she did, so she settled in, not moving until he did. "I love you, babe," he told her finally. "I will cherish it. Never doubt it. It was hard fought but deserved. Several of us on the Team got the same award at the same time."

Julie knew he wouldn't say anything more about it, but she reveled in the fact that he had turned *to* her for comfort, rather than away.

A few seconds later he prodded her off his lap and pushed the big box to her. "Maybe not as emotional, but I hope you enjoy it."

Julie tugged at the misaligned paper, loving that he'd taken the time to wrap everything himself. Even the silver snowflake paper was new. When she revealed the picture on the box, she gasped. Then she ripped the paper away in a frenzy. "This had better not be a box you found on the street to use for my gift."

Gabe laughed, leaning back against the front of the couch. "It's not, I promise. Is that a good machine?"

Julie turned to him incredulously. "Hell, *yes*. I've been looking at these for a while but I couldn't justify spending the money on it. I'm not good enough to use it yet."

"Well," he told her smiling, "now you have motivation to get better."

Julie fell into his arms again. "I can't believe you knew I wanted this."

"Well," he admitted, "I kind of didn't. I mean, I had a vague idea. But I have a new girlfriend that works at Jo-Ann's, and she apparently knew your type very well, though she's never met you. Her name is Kate and she's amazing."

Laughing, Julie tugged him down for a kiss. "Am I going to have to fight her for you?"

"I don't know," Gabe told her, frowning. "I mean, she's every bit of sixty, sixty-five maybe, but she looks like a scrapper. Maybe you should just protect me from here."

He sprawled across the floor, tugging her down over top of him. "Think you have one more Christmas present for me? Maybe?"

Grinning, she leaned down to press her lips to his. "Oh, yes, as a matter of fact I do."

ZEKE

CHAPTER ONE

CHRISTMAS EVE

ZEKE WRAPPED his arm around Ember's shoulders, pulling her to a stop.

"I k-know you're on a mission, but j-just stop for a minute and look around."

With a dreamy grin, she nestled under his arm. "I know. I was talking to Dad about this earlier. I can't believe how very lucky we are... *blessed.*"

Drew played over by the Christmas tree with Mercy, Chad and Lora's little girl. The two of them had their heads together, dark and light. They'd become fast friends, even to the point of sending secret messages to each other via cell phones they'd snagged from their parents.

"I d-d-don't know what they're brewing up, but it looks important."

Ember looked up at him with a grin on her mobile face, and he wondered for the five-millionth time what he'd ever done to deserve her. Her left hand was curled protectively beneath her chin, engagement ring hidden.

Anxiety pressed at him. "Is the r-r-ring okay?"

Ember turned to him and cupped his gnarly face in her

soft palms. She'd never minded his scars. "My ring is beautiful, and exactly right. I would have chosen the very same."

He leaned down to meet her kiss. Normally, he was a
little more sure of himself, but an engagement ring was such
a big thing. "I t-t-took Chad with me to choose. Since he'd al-
al-already done it. Dragged Duncan along with us, t-t-too."

Her dark eyes smiled up at him. He loved how they
creased at the corners when she smiled up at him. Hell, who
was he kidding —he loved everything about her.

"It will take me a little while to get used to it. And I
already worry about the stone. I can't help it."

She shrugged in the cage of his arms and leaned her head
against his chest. Again, Zeke wrapped his arms tighter
around her, wishing they were back home so that they could
celebrate.

"Don't worry about the stone, the ring's insured. Hey,
think we can s-s-sneak back to the office?" he whispered.

Ember looked at him, a scandalized look on her face. "No,
we can't go back to the office," she hissed. "You are so bad!"

But her cheeks had flushed, and he knew if there weren't
thirty other people in the bar she would let him tug her back
there. Happily.

When the party started breaking up, he wasn't too
concerned. It had been a nice party, but the weather was
moving things along. Drew's eyes were heavy lidded, and he
would be a bear in the morning. Actually, since tomorrow
was Christmas, maybe he wouldn't be.

Zeke thought of the work he had to do yet tonight. 'Santa'
had gotten Drew several items that needed to be assembled.
He had at least a couple hours of work ahead of him
tonight… hmmm, maybe his dark-haired elf could help him.

By the time they'd waved everybody out and readied the
bar for the next opening, the night after Christmas, it was
creeping on toward midnight. Drew dragged his feet on the

way to the truck, and was asleep in his booster seat within minutes. When they got to the house, Ember moved to wake him but Zeke shook his head. "I'll carry him in."

Drew didn't make a sound as he was carried into the house and up the stairs to his room. Zeke laid him upon the mattress softly, and he didn't rouse. He pulled the little sneakers off, and the lights in the soles glittered in the dark room as they thumped to the floor.

Zeke shook his head. He'd have killed for kicks like that when he was a kid, no lie.

Ember took care of her son better than she did herself. Her work shoes would fall apart before she bought herself new ones. He understood that she'd gotten used to saving money when she'd been living alone, but jeez.

Drew could sleep in his jeans and T-shirt tonight. More than likely he'd be up in just a few hours anyway. Tucking the Captain America sheets and comforter around him, Zeke pushed to his feet.

Ember passed him in the hallway, grinning up at him as she hauled a black plastic trash bag full of toys toward the front room. He pressed a quick kiss to her lips.

"I'll be down in a m-minute."

She nodded, tiptoeing on down the stairs.

Zeke headed to their bedroom, feeling tiredness dogging at his heels. After working all day, then catering the party, the last thing he wanted to do was stay up for hours putting together crazy ass toys for the boy. He had asked Ember why they had to do it, and not Drew.

"Well, some of them he will want to put together himself, but others he'll want to start playing with right away. Like the bike."

Zeke glanced out the window a little dubiously. He would put the bike together, but he had a feeling Drew wouldn't get a chance to ride it for days yet. The slime-green toboggan

Zeke had gotten him, on the other hand, would be used immediately if the forecast for more than a foot of snow was correct.

He retrieved the bike box from where he'd hidden it in the garage and turned on the forced air heater to warm up the space. Within just a few moments the heat was rolling, and he'd dumped all of the parts onto the concrete floor.

What a freaking mess...

The bike itself ended up being pretty easy to put together. It was the assorted extra plastic parts that made him curse a blue streak. The pieces were supposed to turn the bicycle into a motorcycle wannabe. It did end up being pretty cute, even though it was a trial, and he knew Drew would love it.

Ember ducked her head out the door. "How are things coming on your end?"

He stood, stretching his back. "Okay, I think."

She looked at the small pile of hardware on the floor at his feet. "Are you supposed to have extra bolts like that?"

"Yes," he growled.

"Well, when you bring it inside I'll have something to warm you up."

He looked up at her and wiggled his eyebrows.

She laughed lightly before disappearing inside again.

Zeke sat back down on the stool. There *were* a lot of stray parts. He started going through the directions again. If Drew got hurt because he hadn't read the damn papers right, he'd be pissed at himself.

That was what he'd learned he needed to do as a father. He took his step-dad status very seriously and once he and Ember were married he would start the adoption process. Drew was an amazing little dude. Cute like his mother but a little strong willed, *bullheaded* even, like his granddad. Zeke shook his head with a chuckle. What a combination.

When he wheeled the bike into the house, Ember was

there waiting for him. She grinned when she saw the frustrated look on his face.

"What's wrong?"

He shook his head, unwilling to admit that he hadn't found a place for all the parts he'd had left over. He'd ended up putting them into a little cubby for later. The TBI he'd suffered when he was wounded affected his reading but Drew's safety was more important than his pride. If anything started wobbling on that bike, he'd ask one of the guys at work who was handy to help him rebuild it.

Ember gushed over the bike, as he'd known she would. Hell, he could have put together a damn bow and arrow and she would have gushed, because she was just like that. She supported everything he did and made sure he knew it.

"Do you think he'll l-l-like it?"

She quirked a brow at him. "Are you kidding? I think he'll love it. I think he'll love everything we got him. Well, other than the clothes."

Zeke knew she was probably right, but he still worried. This was his first real Christmas as a dad and he wanted everything to be right.

"Hey," she said, stepping close. She cupped his rough face in her hand. "Why are you stressing? He's *six*. I guarantee you he will have an epic Christmas."

Zeke smiled down at Ember. She was totally right. "Okay. What's next on the list?"

Grinning, she stepped back and held her hands out to her sides in a cute pose. "Me."

A surge of heat rolled through him. "I get to do you?"

She giggled and nodded, reaching back to pull the ponytail holder from her long, dark hair. "I've always had this dream of being unwrapped under the tree by the man I love, my fiancé."

"Well, then," Zeke told her seriously. "I consider it my ssolemn duty to fulfill that wish. How would you l-l-like to be unwrapped? Top to bottom? Bottom to top? I can go slow and unwrap carefully, or just rip all that clothing off q-q-quick."

Ember giggled and turned to toss a blanket and a few pillows on the floor. "I think quick and dirty gets the job done tonight. We're both a little tired."

Zeke widened his eyes, "Oh, I'm fine now."

"There will be a little boy knocking on our door in just a couple of hours, though."

He winced, knowing she was right. Stepping behind her as she flung out the blanket to straighten it, he cradled her against his front. She shivered as he nibbled kisses down her neck. He reached around her front and started unbuttoning buttons, but she stilled his hands. Turning in his arms she whipped the shirt up and over her head. Zeke automatically looked down, then blew out a breath in surprise. *Wow*, her tits looked fucking awesome in that pretty green bra. "Can we leave this on? You look like a m-m-illion bucks in this."

Ember grinned, brushing her breasts against his chest. "You like this, huh?"

Zeke cupped her hips, letting her feel the instant erection she'd sprung him into.

"Oh, yeah..."

Even as tired as he'd been a couple of minutes ago, his heart began to thud heavily in his chest. Ember got his blood going like no one else ever had. Or ever would.

Zeke knew she was the woman for him, he had known it for a year now. It had been easy to give her the engagement ring earlier tonight. Actually, once he'd gotten the thing in his hands three months ago, it had been hard to keep it from her. But he was glad he had waited until tonight. Proposing in front of all their friends would be a memory they'd both cherish.

The metal on her finger was cool as she cupped his rough face. "I love you," she whispered.

"I love you too, babe."

She spun away from him, hips swaying back and forth as she crooked a finger at him to follow. Which he did, with a laugh and smile, unbuttoning his flannel shirt as he walked. Her eyes heated as he began to undress, and he loved that fire in her eyes. Never would he have imagined seeing that look on a woman's face again. After he'd been blown up in Iraq, his face mangled by the concrete wall, he hadn't been comfortable out in public. His looks had changed drastically.

This past year he'd decided that he was about done with the reconstructive surgeries. They were so stressful, not just physically, but mentally and emotionally as well; and not just for him but for Ember and Drew, too. He was pretty content with where he was now. No, he'd never win any beauty pageants, but he appealed to the only woman that mattered. And Drew didn't seem to care at all, though the boy had to recognize how different he was from other dads.

Ember stopped in the doorway of the living room and posed, hips cocked, breasts up. God, she was gorgeous. Her dark hair fell around her shoulders.

Zeke drew close and reached out to run a finger over the swell of her right breast. She backed away from his touch and glanced pointedly above her. A small sprig of mistletoe had been hung from the doorjamb.

"Did you d-do this?" he laughed.

He knew she had, but he loved the playful expression that lightened her face. "I did. I want to start some new traditions just for us. And I know that in general it's just a nuisance plant, but it's meant to be a good luck charm for a long married life."

He smiled at her. "I think it's a fabulous idea."

Reaching out, he wrapped her in his arms. "I love you,

Ember, you are my whole world. I know I tell you th-th-that all the time, but I really m-mean it."

"I know you do, babe."

The acceptance and encouragement in her eyes fed his soul like nothing else could. And the need he could see in her expression encouraged his body. Zeke finished unbuttoning his flannel shirt, and dropped it to the floor. Then he did the same with the T-shirt he wore beneath.

"Are you sure little man is out?"

She grinned at him, her straight white teeth gleaming in the shine from the Christmas tree lights. "Totally. And Dad won't be over till later tomorrow. He's staying with Karen."

Zeke leaned back to peer down into her eyes. "How do you feel about that? Seems kind of sudden to me."

Ember smiled, her eyes calm. "I think it's fine. I know they haven't been together long, but they seem right together. He's been alone for a long time, and it seems only fair that if my life is evolving his should be able to as well."

Yes, that was very true. In the past year their lives had changed dramatically. And Hank's had, too. Hank had snapped around Christmas time last year, sending Ember to the hospital after hitting her in the fog of a flashback. It nearly broke her heart to do it but Ember had him arrested, it had been the best thing she could have done. Hank had gone to jail for a couple of days, then the judge sentenced him to counseling for his PTSD. And over the course of the year, Zeke had seen him change into a different man. Hank laughed more and seemed open to everything. His relationship with Ember had blossomed, as well as with his grandson Drew. Zeke felt privileged to be a part of his healing.

The relationship with Karen had kind of come out of the blue, though. Hank had come home from the bar one night and said that he'd met someone. He'd been flushed and sweating, but there had been a masculine excitement in his eyes that was undeniable. Like Hank, Karen was a Vietnam Vet herself, having served in the Army as a nurse in the field hospitals. She was a calm, solid woman with a playful streak that balanced Hank out perfectly. It seemed very natural that they were together; like Zeke and Ember, they *fit*.

Now, Hank had practically moved in with her.

Karen's grown children were coming home for Christmas, and this was the first chance they would have to meet Hank. His father-in-law to be was looking forward to meeting her family but a little nervous, too. Zeke hoped all went well for them.

So, their house was quiet – their little mouse was all snug in his bed, and Zeke had a beautiful, half dressed woman right in front of him. He glanced up at the mistletoe. "I'll kiss you under the m-m-mistletoe, but I don't think it will matter. I plan on having a l-long, loving life with you for many years to come — the rest of my life."

Ember's expression softened. "I know you do. It's not like I'm ever going to let you go," she laughed.

He took her mouth in a seductive kiss and gathered her into his arms. Ember was the best armful of anything he'd ever held. As she looped her arms up around his shoulders, her breasts pressed into him even harder.

Need surged through Zeke. He reached down, cupped her delicious ass in his broad palms and lifted her up to eye level, grinding his erection into her. "There. We've sealed this mistletoe deal before Santa caught us."

Giggling, she shivered in his arms, her thighs widening to accommodate him. "Take me to the couch," she whispered.

Zeke thought that was a damn good idea. Turning with her in his arms, he went to the couch and lowered them down onto it, Ember still straddling his hips. With a quick kiss she pushed away from his heavy chest and stood before him to wiggle out of her jeans. Then, with a saucy pose, she

J.M. MADDEN

shimmied out of her panties. She let him look for a long moment, then walked toward him with a sway in her hips.

Zeke unbuttoned, then unzipped his fly, pushing his jeans down his hips but not off. He still wore his boots, but he didn't want to take the time to remove them.

Ember pushed his knees apart and lowered herself to the floor in front of him, looking at him up the length of his body. Anticipation slammed through him. He knew where this was going and the thought of the pleasure he was about to feel whipped through him.

Yup. There she goes.

Ember pulled his underwear away and wrapped her mouth around him in one smooth movement. Zeke was glad he was sitting down because all of the blood left his head in a rush, heading south.

To her mouth.

It was epic.

Damn. Rocking his head back against the couch, he looked at the ceiling, counting peaks of stucco. He needed to do something to try to control his response to her talented mouth, otherwise this was not going to last long. They were a year into their relationship, and he still responded to her as if this was their first time, *every time.* Ember had admitted that it was the same for her, this excitement and wonder.

Maybe because they kept doing things like this.

Ember wanted him focused. With a squeeze, she made him look down at her.

"Do you know how much I love you?" he asked her, his voice gruff.

She quirked a brow at him, as if to say *'you'd better',* and he chuckled. Then she did something with her fingers under his balls and he lost all coherent thought. He could feel the orgasm building fast, but he let her go until he was right on the edge. Then, clutching her upper arms, he pulled her up into a kiss.

Ember moaned at not being able to finish him, but he didn't plan on letting her be disappointed long. "You can f-f-f-finish me in a minute."

Leaning forward into the kiss, her wrapped one arm around her back to keep her still, then felt down around his bunched jeans until he found her silky skin where she leaned into him. She gasped against his mouth as his fingers travelled down, pausing at the small patch of hair at the apex of her thighs. Then, very carefully, he pushed down further, using one finger to part her wet folds.

She moaned as he brushed over the focus of her pleasure, the little bundle of flesh so small beneath his big, male fingers. Zeke had practiced bringing her to climax this way many times. It was an art, this gentle manipulation. With the smallest of movements he began to pet that tiny little bundle of awesomeness.

Apparently, he was mastering the art of pleasing her pretty well. Ember tried to pull her mouth away, but he kept her tight to him, kissing her thoroughly as he continued to ever so carefully direct her body. She gasped and began to pant, her hands coming up to clutch his face as her body surged against his hand. Zeke felt her abs contracting against him as she worked herself against his hard finger.

Their mouths still touched, but they were merely breathing each other in as her pleasure built. And when she did that high, little cry of release and her body began to convulse against him, melting into his hand, he took her mouth to swallow that cry. He had given her that pleasure, and he felt justified to take it inside himself.

Ember sagged in his arms, but her slight weight was never a burden. Rather, it was a gift that she gave him, that trust.

He let her catch her breath for a few seconds, but his body demanded release. When he shifted, she seemed to know what he wanted. Cupping her ass in his strong hands, he lifted her up as he shifted his hips to the edge of the couch. Then he set her down perfectly over his straining cock.

Her orgasm had left her sopping wet, and as that heat enveloped him, he clenched his teeth to keep from crying out. Ember braced her hands on his chest and shifted once up and down before a secondary orgasm rippled through her.

Zeke did gasp then, because he felt every tiny wave as her body tightened around him. Hands clenching on her hips, he pulled her down against him. They were skin to skin, almost bone to bone, they were so tight and Ember began to grind against him.

Zeke dragged in another breath, his big hands on her hips, controlling her movements instinctively. But she had a goal she was working toward, he could feel it. She wanted another orgasm.

Tilting her pelvis forward, more in line with his own, he positioned her so that every movement rocked her clit against his hardness.

Unfortunately, what felt good for her felt just as good for him, and the ball of heat and expectation in his groin built to the point he couldn't contain it any more. With a mighty lunge, muscles straining, teeth bared, he let the pleasure take him over.

Ember cried out as she felt his release and he thought he felt her come again as well, but his mind had gone blank. Then he heard her cry out, and she was tightening around his cock once more.

Oh, fuck...

For several minutes, they just panted and drew oxygen

back into their lungs. Ember curled up on his chest and he wrapped his arms around her, happy to have her on his heart.

"Merry Christmas to me," she whispered. Then she looked around, a little dazed. "Guess we didn't need the blanket and pillows."

Zeke blinked and glanced down at the pile of bedding on the floor that they hadn't gotten to. "Nope."

Then, gathering his strength, he pushed up from the couch, setting Ember gently on her feet. While she headed to the bathroom to clean up, he gathered their scattered clothes and tossed them to the laundry room floor before heading to the master bathroom. Ember's gaze lifted to his as he stripped off the rest of his clothing and climbed into the shower with her.

"I love you," he told her softly, gathering her to his heart.

"And I love you," she whispered back.

CHAPTER TWO

DREW WAITED to a respectable six thirty before springing onto the bed between them and announcing that he had been waiting on them to get up for *hours*.

He hadn't, of course, but to a six-year-old, minutes probably did feel like hours on Christmas Day.

Ember stretched slowly, pretending to be especially tired.

Or maybe she wasn't pretending. They had been … energetic last night.

Zeke grinned and rolled out of bed, glad that Ember had suggested he put sleep clothes. No need to teach Drew more than he needed to know about life on this Christmas morning.

Finally, giggling at Drew's desperation, Ember rolled out of bed and followed.

Zeke knew she would be right there in the thick of ripping off paper and exploring. Her birthday had been in October, so he'd already gotten a glimpse of the way her enthusiasm took over. Christmas wrapping paper was shredded, and all that careful wrapping *obliterated* as the room echoed with squeals. It was like she regressed to being a ten-year-old kid, gushing and exclaiming over everything he received. Zeke had to laugh, because she had bought almost everything there.

Drew loved the bike they had gotten him, and kept returning to it between unwrapping other gifts. More than once, Zeke saw him glance outside. The snow was still falling softly but steadily. They'd gotten almost a foot overnight. There would be no biking today.

"I th-think it may have to wait until we can clear a s-s-sidewalk, buddy."

"I know," he sighed. "Can I keep it in my room?"

"No," Ember told him calmly. "Bikes go in garages."

"But Mom," Drew said. "*Dirty* bikes go in garages. This one is brand new and clean."

She blinked, her expression turning thoughtful. "You're right, Drew. It can stay in your room until you ride it outside, then it has to stay in the garage. Deal?"

"Deal!"

He jumped into her arms, giving her a neck-cracking hug. Then he turned to Zeke and did the same thing before heading back to the wreckage under the tree.

Ember walked over to him and he opened his arms automatically. This had become a favorite position of theirs, curled together on the same piece of furniture.

"You did good, babe," he whispered, voice soft.

Ember nodded a little. "I think so. The bike is the hit, though. Well done!"

Zeke grinned and dropped a kiss to her dark hair. In response, she dropped her head to his chest, lightly kissing his neck, before tucking under his jaw.

～

EMBER COULDN'T IMAGINE A MORE perfect Christmas. Zeke's

heart beat strongly beneath her cheek and his massive arms cradled her like she was the most precious thing in the world to him.

The light glinted on the stone of the engagement ring he'd bought her. She'd kind of expected the ring months ago, but he'd never popped the question. She understood why now, though. He'd wanted to do it while all of his friends and LNF work family were present. Zeke's real family certainly wouldn't have come out for the holiday or the excitement of an engagement.

Ember understood about having a work ethic, but damn. They'd flown out to meet his family once, and the difference in lifestyles was very evident. His parents loved Zeke, but they just didn't understand why he needed to be away from home on the family farm. Right in front of her, his mother asked him why he stayed out there 'so far from home'.

She sighed, running her hand over his chest. There was nothing they could do about it now. He and his family just didn't see eye to eye. They loved him, but they just didn't understand him anymore. He'd made his own life in Denver, the job at Lost and Found and the friends there who'd become family even before he and Ember had gotten together last year. Now, he was going to have a wife, son, father-in-law and no doubt more kids somewhere along the way.

Drew looked up to show them something, and Ember's heart almost burst with pride. Her little man was growing up so fast. He'd started Kindergarten this year and already seemed to be charming the teachers. He needed another haircut already… and his feet suddenly seemed to be so big!

One of the boxes he received was full of clothes, a size larger than he wore now. Looking at the pjs flashing his ankles, she was extra glad she'd done that. Poor kid was outgrowing things faster than he could wear them out.

Her little man…

And her big man…

She looked up at Zeke. His bright, ice blue eyes connected with hers in shared joy and love. Ember couldn't ever remember feeling so fulfilled. Zeke had become everything to her and Drew.

In the past year, he'd become a parent and live-in partner. They'd moved out of the apartment and into a house not too far from her dad's. Drew stayed in the same school district and the drive to LNF and Frog Dog was an equal distance away from home. It had been a little strange buying a house before they were married, but the realtor had shrugged and told them it was no big deal anymore.

Ember kind of wished the woman had urged Zeke to marry her, but it hadn't happened. Stretching her hand out, she looked at the ring again. It sparkled in the light, and seemed very natural there on her finger, like it was meant to be there. The men had chosen well.

Sometime soon, she would broach the subject of *when*…

As soon as the day lightened, Drew wanted to go outside and go sled riding. There was a park less than a block away that had a decent hill on one side of it. Maybe that would be enough for him.

After gulping down some pancakes and bacon, all three of them bundled up to go outside.

The snow was actually too powdery for good sledding, but Drew was set on trying out the new toboggan. And when Zeke looked into the boy's brown eyes, eyes that looked so much like his mother's, there was no denying him.

When they got to the park, other kids had apparently had the same idea. The snow was already packed down on the hill and judging by the kids at the bottom, it appeared to be fast.

"I don't know if this is a good idea," Ember muttered. "Those kids look older than Drew."

"I th-think it'll be all right, they're grade school kids, not high school or anything."

Zeke was attacked by a case of nerves, though. His ugly, scarred mug was probably not what kids wanted to see on Christmas morning. "M-m-maybe you should g-go up with him."

Ember stopped and looked at him. "Why?"

He grimaced at her and wondered if he needed to say it out loud.

"Oh," she said softly.

He hated that sound. It was like she was humoring him or something, or pitying him. No, in his mind he knew she didn't, but she didn't always know how to deal with his tendency to stay in the background. Though he was generally okay with being in public, this might be a little too much exposure for his comfort level.

"I d-d-don't want D-drew picked on because of m-m-me."

Her eyes softened and she nodded slowly. "Okay, if that's how you feel."

She took the nylon cord from his hand and started walking up the hill. "Come on, Drew. Let's test this baby out!"

Drew looked back at Zeke in disappointment. "I thought Zeke was going to go with me."

"He'll catch you at the bottom," Ember promised, lifting a brow at Zeke.

He nodded, hearing the warning in her voice.

"I'll g-get you at the bottom, b-buddy. Promise."

That seemed to appease Drew. Running up the hill ahead of his mother, he kept looking back to make sure she was coming. He slipped and fell on his face once, then bounced right back up, giggling. There was enough snow on the ground that he probably couldn't be hurt.

Just then, one of the older boys came screaming down the hill and wiped out at the bottom. Zeke suddenly had second thoughts about sending the two people he loved the most up the hill to hurtle down it on a quarter-inch thick piece of plastic. What the hell had he been thinking?

A sled flew free from its owner and glided toward Zeke. Putting out a booted foot he caught the purple projectile and handed it back to the kid running after it. A red-cheeked boy of about nine or ten said "Thanks!" then looked up at Zeke with a smile that slowly faded into surprise as he cocked his head to the side.

Yup. There it was. That lovely, stupefied look people got on their faces when they couldn't decide what to do when they saw him. He knew it would happen. Now the boy would either cringe or gasp—maybe both—before he ran away.

But the boy did neither. He held out his hand like a little gentleman and smiled up at Zeke excitedly.

"You're Drew's dad, right? He talks about you a *lot*, like all the time. He's in my little sister's class at school."

Zeke took the boy's gloved hand, blinking in surprise. "H-h-he does? He is?"

"Oh, yeah," the kid nodded. "He told us you're this awesome Marine and how you went to war in Afghanistan, but you got injured. Nice to meet you, I'm Adam. Our dad's in the Army. He's over there fighting now." The boy smiled up at Zeke, his face open and friendly.

Zeke let go of the boy's hand, shocked at the easy acceptance on the kid's face, and in his words. Drew had talked about him to his friends at school. And called him *Dad*.

"When he gets b-back I'd l-l-like to meet him," Zeke told the kid.

Adam nodded as he started back up the slope. "Yeah, he should be back in a few months. Gotta go again!"

Zeke watched the boy run up the hill, dragging his sled behind him.

He heard familiar laughter and turned to see Drew and Ember flying down the hill toward him. Adjusting his position, he squared himself in case he needed to catch them, but they glided to a stop right in front of him. Snow had sprayed up and all over Drew's face, and he giggled as he wiped it away. Ember's grin was so broad it looked like it would split her face. She huffed out a laugh as he pulled her up into his arms.

Then her gaze sharpened on his face. He probably did look a little dazed, he still felt a little dazed, to be honest. Shaking his head, he pressed a kiss to her lips. "I'm okay. G-g-gonna go sled with my son. I'll t-t-talk to you about it later."

Ember's eyes filled with tears and she nodded, a dazzling smile lighting up her face as she looked at him.

Drew looked shocked when Zeke held out his hand, but clambered to his feet happily. "You're going to take me now? Really?"

"Yup. Is th-that all right? Do you m-m-mind if the kids see me?"

Drew looked at him, head cocked in confusion. "Yeah, it's all right! I don't mind if the kids see you. You're my dad. I want *everybody* to know you're my dad." Then Drew smiled up at Zeke with the same dazzling look on his face as Ember and Zeke's heart turned over in his chest.

His throat closed tight at the matter-of-fact way Drew said it and he had to nod in reply as they started walking up the hill. If it was that easy for Drew to accept him, he needed to be the man the boy thought he was and the father Drew needed him to be.

With a final glance back at Ember, they marched up the slope together.

He cocked an eye at the sled that had looked plenty big in the store but suddenly seemed awfully short and narrow. Well, all he had to do now was see if he could fit his six foot six ass on the damned thing. Kids would sure be talking about something other than his looks if they crashed and burned. But as he wrapped his arms around Drew to keep his son safe as they hurtled down the hill, he couldn't imagine a more perfect day.

The End...

THE LOST AND FOUND SERIES

If you would like to read about the 'combat modified' veterans of the **Lost and Found Investigative Service**, check out these books:

The Embattled Road (FREE prequel)
Duncan, John and Chad

Embattled Hearts-Book 1 (FREE)
John and Shannon

Embattled Minds-Book 2
Zeke and Ember

Embattled Home-Book 3
Chad and Lora

Embattled SEAL- Book 4
Harper and Cat

Embattled Ever After- Book 5
Duncan and Alex

Her Forever Hero- Grif
Grif and Kendall

SEAL's Lost Dream-Flynn
Flynn and Willow

Unbreakable SEAL- Max
Max and Lacey

Embattled Christmas

Reclaiming The Seal
Gabe and Julie

Loving Lilly
Diego and Lilly

Her Secret Wish
Rachel and Dean

Other books by J.M. Madden
A Touch of Fae
Second Time Around
A Needful Heart
Wet Dream
Love on the Line
The Billionaire's Secret Obsession
The Awakening Society- FREE
Tempt Me

If you'd like to connect with me on social media and keep updated on my releases, try these links:

Newsletter

Website

Facebook

Twitter

And of course you can always email me at authorjmmadden@gmail.com

About the Author~

NY Times and USA Today Bestselling author J.M. Madden writes compelling romances between 'combat modified' military men and the women who love them. J.M. Madden loves any and all good love stories, most particularly her own. She has two beautiful children and a husband who always keeps her on her toes.

J.M. was a Deputy Sheriff in Ohio for nine years, until hubby moved the clan to Kentucky. When not chasing the family around, she's at the computer, reading and writing, perfecting her craft. She occasionally takes breaks to feed her animal horde and is trying to control her office-supply addiction, but both tasks are uphill battles. Happily, she is writing full-time and always has several projects in the works. She also dearly loves to hear from readers! So, drop her a line. She'll respond.

OTHER BOOKS BY J.M. MADDEN

A Touch of Fae

Second Time Around

A Needful Heart

Wet Dream

Love on the Line

The Billionaire's Secret Obsession

The Awakening Society- FREE

Tempt Me

And of course you can always email me at
authorjmmadden@gmail.com